CURRICULUM COLLECTION
TEACHER MEDIA CENTER
JEWISH EDUCATION CENTER
OF CLEVELAND
2030 South Taylor Road
Cleveland Heights, Ohio 44118

RMC	Batterman, Lee Chai'ah
973.4	Two cents and a milk
BAT	bottle

11237

Two Cents and a Milk Bottle

Two Cents
and a
Milk Bottle

Lee Chai`ah Batterman

Illustrated by James Wattling

ALEF DESIGN GROUP

Library of Congress Cataloging-in-Publication Data
Batterman, Lee Chai`ah, 1926–
  Two cents and a milk bottle / Lee Chai`ah Batterman ; illustrated by James Wattling.
    p.   c.m.
  Summary: In 1937 twelve-year-old Leely and her financially struggling Jewish family more one more time into yet another New York neighborhood where they begin a new life.
  ISBN 1-881283-18-6
  [1. Jews--New York (N.Y.)--Juvenile fiction. 2. Jews--New York (N.Y.)--Fiction. 3. Family Life--Fiction.] I. Wattling, James, ill. II. Title.
  PZ7.B32437Tw 1997
  [Fic]--dc21   97-12092
                                                                           CIP
                                                                            AC

Any resemblance to people dead or alive is strictly coincidental.

ISBN 1-881283-18-6
Copyright © 1997 Lee Chai`ah Batterman
Illustrations Copyright © 1997 James Wattling
Published by Alef Design Group
All rights reserved. No part of this publication may be reproduced or transmitted in any form or by any means graphic, electronic or mechanical, including photocopying, recording or by any information storage and retrieval system, without permission in writing from the publisher.

ALEF DESIGN GROUP • 4423 FRUITLAND AVENUE, LOS ANGELES, CA 90058
(800) 845–0662 • (213) 582–1200 • (213) 585–0327 FAX
HTTP://WWW.ALEFDESIGN.COM

MANUFACTURED IN THE UNITED STATES OF AMERICA

Dedication

This book
is dedicated
to my grandchildren.
May they learn
to know and love
their heritage.

Acknowledgements

Without the inspiration of Esther Gropper Feldman, this book would not have materialized. I am grateful to her for turning on the light and for showing me the path.

In memory of Jean Shirley for her friendship and encouragement.

To Rabbi David Goldstein I extend my gratitude for his guidance, direction, and patience.

I thank my husband, David, for his sacrifices and understanding.

Table of Contents

Foreword 9
1 Roll Out the Barrel 12
2 Kenubble Trouble 25
3 New Friends 33
4 The Bike Lesson 41
5 Going into Business 56
6 Mr. Piccolo 67
7 Black and Blue All Over 77
8 Bar Mitzvah Class 82
9 Murder and Dead 94
10 Middle C 103
11 Best Friends 113
12 The Bonfire 125
13 Bad News 138
14 Good News 151
15 The Miracle 160
16 Finally 173
17 Wrapped and Ready 181
18 Act of Repentance 190
19 The Hanukkah Party 198
20 The Aftermath 213
Glossary 217

Foreword

MEET TWELVE-YEAR-OLD LEELY DORMAN, HER FIFTEEN-YEAR-old sister, Evy, and Arnie, her seven-year-old brother. They are children of Jewish immigrants from Russia who left poverty and persecution behind and brought with them their traditions, expressions, and humor when they came to Brooklyn, New York. This is where the three siblings were born.

The year is 1937, one of the worst years of the Great Depression. Leely and Evy help their mother by washing clothes in a tub and hanging them up to dry on a clothesline outside their tenement apartment window.

For a nickel Mama rode a street car, Papa made a phone call, and the children bought extra large ice cream cones. For ten cents Leely went to the movies, and for three cents Evy bought a stamp to mail a letter. Arnie got a few marbles for only one penny, or bubble gum wrapped with a baseball card that he flipped and traded with friends.

It is a time before television, computers, tape decks, Nintendo, and McDonald's. And, yet the Dorman family is happy.

Two Cents and a Milk Bottle

1 *Roll Out the Barrel*

"LEELY DORMAN, YOU'RE WANTED IN THE PRINCIPAL'S OFFICE!" Mrs. Weber said in front of the whole classroom.

I froze in my seat. In all my six years of school I had never been called into the principal's office. I remained glued to my seat, twisting a long curl that hung on my shoulder.

"Well, come on child, move!"

I raised myself, but getting my legs to work was like pulling taffy. "Should I take my books with me?" I didn't know why I was being called away.

"Take all your things—sweater, lunch, everything."

I dragged myself to the front of the room and, with a quivering voice, said, "I didn't do anything wrong, Mrs. Weber. Honest."

Mrs. Weber smiled warmly at me. "I don't think there's anything for you to worry about, Leely." She handed me a folded sheet of paper. "Take this with you."

But I did worry. All kinds of thoughts raced through my head as I walked down the hall. When I arrived at the principal's office the secretary, Miss Owens, looked at me with a what-do-you-want expression on her face.

"I'm Leely Dorman." My voice creaked like an old door.

"Oh, yes! The Dorman girl. Leave all your books on my desk, please." She took the folded sheet of paper Mrs. Weber had given me and slid it into a manila envelope that already had my name on it. "Here," she said. Yyour brother's transfer is in here, too. Good luck!"

"Transfer? Where am I going? What should I do with it?" I asked.

"Don't you know?" Miss Owens raised her brows and looked at the other secretary. "You're moving! Your mother called and said for you to leave school immediately. I couldn't quite understand her Yiddish accent, but I did get something about hurrying home to pack before the movers come."

I was stunned. Mama hadn't mentioned anything about moving this morning. Yet I had heard her tell Papa that she preferred to move on lucky days, Monday or Thursday. But I had heard that many times before, so I didn't pay attention to it. Now we were moving again. Oh, gosh! How I hated it! It meant making new friends, feeling strange in a new class, and getting acquainted with a new neighborhood.

I felt embarrassed that I didn't know anything about it. I looked away to hide my tears.

"Where's my brother?" I asked.

"We've sent for him, too." Miss Owens noticed my tears and

confused expression. She looked into my face. "Leely, is your mother at home?"

"No, she's working at my father's butcher store."

"Well, do you know how to pack a house for moving?"

I gave a deep sigh. "Oh, yes! My older sister Evy and I have had plenty of experience in packing. We move almost every year."

Miss Owens nodded toward the envelope in my hand and remarked, "I should think so, judging from all the transfers in that envelope." I squirmed and bit my lip.

Arnie came walking in holding the hand of a monitor who had brought him from his first grade class. His sweater was half on and half off. He looked at me questioningly.

"We have to go home, Arnie. We're moving again," I said as I slipped his sweater back on his body.

"Again? Where are we moving to now?" he asked.

"I don't know." I shot a quick look at Miss Owens and felt my face get hot. She was shaking her head. "Tsk, tsk, tsk."

I grabbed Arnie's arm. "Come on Arnie, let's go." As we left the office I heard Miss Owens say to the other secretary, "They're probably being dispossessed." I didn't know what dispossessed meant, but I did know I didn't like the sound of it. I felt ashamed and hurried out.

I held Arnie's hand as we quickly ran across the streets to avoid oncoming trolley cars and honking automobiles. Most of the automobiles looked alike: dark-colored boxes on skinny rubber tires. The drivers played with their horns as if they were toys. Beep, beep. Beep, beep.

"Why are we moving again, Leely?" Arnie ran to keep up with me.

"I'm sure it's for the same reason we always move—to live near Papa's new store."

We were at the corner when I heard my name called from behind me. I turned. There was my older sister Evy, running and waving to us with a manila envelope in her hand. "Wait up!" she called. We waited.

She arrived, panting. "How do you like that? We're moving again!" Evy caught her breath. "Mama never mentioned we were going to move today. Something must have happened!"

"Yeah, I know," I said. "And Mama wants us to start packing immediately."

As we hurried down the street Evy opened her envelope. "Evy!" I shouted. "You're not supposed to look at your school records!"

"I know, I know, but I'm curious to see what grades I got."

"Why bother looking? You know they're gonna be A's." I peeked at the sheet with her and nodded my head. "See, what did I tell you? They're always A's."

Not only was Evy an "A" student, but she also had a large vocabulary. She carried a dictionary with her all the time and memorized new words each day. Her friends nicknamed her Dickie (short for dictionary), and we called her Dickie whenever we needed a definition for a word.

"Dickie, what does diz-po-zess mean?" I asked as we continued down the long block to our house.

"It means to take away something from someone, so they no longer own it. Why do you ask?"

"Well, as we left the principal's office I heard Miss Owens say, 'They're probably being diz-po-zessed.' It sounded bad, even if I didn't know what it meant."

Evy thought for a moment. "The dispossess she meant was eviction. When the landlord removes the tenants from the apartment he rented to them and puts them out into the street. Furniture and all."

Arnie skipped backwards in front of Evy. "Remember that family we once saw sitting on their furniture outside in the street? Remember they were crying because they couldn't pay their rent and had nowhere to sleep? You mean like them?"

Evy and I looked at each other, and without saying a word we increased our pace almost to a run. Evy stretched her neck to look down the block. "I think somebody is sitting on the stoop."

Arnie ran ahead of us to see who it was. He stopped short as soon as he recognized the person, then raced back to tell us. "It's our landlord, Mr. Chiznik!"

Evy grabbed Arnie's hand. "Let's stick together. If he says anything to us, we won't answer. We'll just walk up the steps and into the house."

We approached the house marching like three soldiers on parade, ignoring Mr. Chiznik's angry look and his grumbling. He waved a paper in the air and hollered, "This is your eviction notice. I'm dispossessing you! My moving men will be here soon, and they're going to put your furniture in the street!"

We didn't stop or even side-glance at the landlord. We stomped up the steps in a tight group, opened the front door, and slammed it shut behind us.

While waiting for Evy to unlock the inner door I had the same embarrassed feeling I had had in the school office. I was glad nobody had heard what Mr. Chiznik said. I opened the door again and poked my head out. "No, you won't dispossess us either, because we're gonna pack and move first. So there!" I shut the door with a bang and ran up the flight of steps to our apartment.

Once upstairs we found four empty moving barrels standing in the foyer and a stack of newspapers piled on the floor. Stretched out on the newspapers was Malkah, our cat. Malkah was all white except for a silver spot that crowned her forehead. Malkah means "queen" in the Yiddish language, and Malkah acted like a queen. She carried herself with pride and was always primping. Evy said she was majestic. No hard floors for Malkah; she found the softest chairs and slept in Arnie's bed. She was beautiful—and she knew it.

Evy said, "Joe, Papa's moving man, was here. Papa must have given him the key to deliver the barrels."

"What's 'the key to the liver,' Evy?" Arnie always mispronounced words. Sometimes he gave them humorous meanings. Arnie's innocent blue eyes were wide open. He looked cute, even though Papa had had his blond curls cut when he went into kindergarten. Also, Arnie finally got to wear knickers. This made him feel like a big boy.

"Deliver, Arnie, de-li-ver. Papa gave Joe the key to our house so he could de-li-ver, bring the barrels here," Evy carefully explained, as she always did. "Mama and Papa trust Joe."

"I should think so!" I said. "After all these years of moving Papa's

fixtures from one store to another and our furniture from one house to another."

Evy shoved Malkah off the stack of newspapers. "Okay, enough talking. Let's get started," she said with authority. "Arnie, start tearing these newspapers in half. Leely, you empty the clothes closets."

I laid our clothes out on the beds and wrapped the sheets around them the way Mama wrapped thin *blintze* pancakes after she filled them with cheese. I folded the top over, the bottom over, then rolled one side over the other. I called out, "Hey, Evy, you should see how neatly I packed the clothes. They look like cheese in a *blintze*. A giant *blintze!*"

"No playing around, Leely. Come on! We have to work very fast." And I did. The two closets and the large wardrobe were emptied and "*blintzed*" in no time at all. Then I went into the kitchen to help Evy with the dishes.

Arnie crushed paper and stuffed it into the spaces in the barrel. He was having a conversation with Evy. "So how come we're moving again if it isn't even a year since we moved into this house?"

"Because this butcher store turned out to be worse than the one Papa had before," Evy answered.

"Yeah, it never turns out to be the gold mine Papa always dreams of." I removed pots and pans from the cabinet. "I wonder where this store is. I hope it's back in the last neighborhood we lived in. I like that one best."

"It's not. I think Papa mentioned it's in Crown Heights." Evy placed the wrapped glasses in the barrel. She pointed to show Arnie where to stuff the paper around them.

I put small pots into larger ones and filled them with small kitchen utensils. "Where is Crown Heights?" I asked.

"I don't know. Another section of Brooklyn we never lived in. Another public school we never went to." Evy closed her eyes and bit the side of her lip. This usually meant she was thinking. But this time there were tears running down her cheeks. She placed her hands on her hips. Her hair, which she had rolled in curlers and slept on all night, was now hanging straight. "Do you know this is the seventh public school I've attended?"

"And it's my fifth." I lined the layers of dishes with linens.

Arnie shook his head rapidly, eager to be part of his older sisters' grievances. "So I'm only in first grade, and already I'll be in my second school."

"Hey, kids! We'd better work faster if we want to be ready when Joe gets here," Evy said to prod us along.

"I hope he gets here before Mr. Chiznik's men do," I said. "Evy, why does he want to dispossess us? Do you think Papa didn't pay the rent?"

"Could be," Evy answered. "I know Papa was angry each morning he had to go down to the cellar to shovel coal into the furnace so the house would be warm when we woke up."

"And Mama, too," I added. "Whenever Papa had to leave in the middle of the night to go to the slaughterhouse, Mama had to shovel the coal. She didn't like it either."

"And how about when Papa had to go out to buy coal because Mr. Chiznik never had the coal bin filled?" Evy stopped for a moment. "I bet that was why Papa didn't pay the rent. I remember him saying that Chiznik now owed us money."

Evy and I worked quickly to get everything packed. Arnie was helpful, too. He followed orders without complaining. That is, until we gave him the iron to pack in the bottom of the barrel. He refused. "Oh, no! I'm not gonna get lost in a barrel again."

We laughed, remembering when we had moved the last time. Arnie had fallen asleep at the bottom of a barrel. Not knowing he was in there, we tossed pillows and blankets in, covering him completely. When he awoke and started crying we looked all over the house but couldn't find him. Arnie was frightened; he didn't know where he was. We were frightened because we couldn't find him. It was scary but funny.

The door opened downstairs, and there was a rush of footsteps and voices coming up the stairs. Mama was in the lead, and Joe and his helpers were behind.

Mama called out, *"Kinder*! Children! We're here! Did you pack everything?" Mama looked like she had had a busy day. The crescent comb at the side of her straight brown hair was slipping out. She carried cardboard cartons.

"Of course, everything," Evy and I said together.

"What are the boxes for?" Evy asked.

"For the miz-lanyus and medicine chest, what else?" Mama answered.

"They're packed," I said, and I thrust my chest out proudly.

"We put the medicine into pots and the miscellaneous into paper bags," Evy added.

"*Nu*, good! Then we'll put in the boxes, from the ice box the food, and from the cabinets the groceries. Joe, we have to move fast, it's Friday. The Sabbath comes at sundown, and we have to be in the new house before." Mama shook her head, annoyed. "This is why I don't like to move on Friday." She looked under the blankets we had put on top of the packed barrels.

Joe greeted us with his usual Italian-style kiss, one on each cheek. As always, he wore his gray uniform that matched his pepper-and-salt hair. He wrapped rope around each barrel and, as though they were feathers, his men lifted the barrels onto their bent backs. Slowly they trudged down the stairs.

Fascinated, I watched as they skillfully turned and twisted the big, bulky dining room furniture through the doorways.

Mama looked through the cabinets and closets to make sure we had packed everything. She smiled. "You're good children. I can depend on you." She hugged and kissed Evy and me.

Arnie cried out, "What about me? I helped, too! I'm a good boy!"

"*Oy vey!* Of course you, too, *Tatele*, darling. You're the best boy I have!"

Suddenly there was a hullabaloo outside. We ran to the front windows to see what the noise was about. Mr. Chiznik's movers had arrived and were arguing with him. Mr. Chiznik was shouting, "No, I won't pay you. You came too late. Now they're moving out themselves."

One of the movers hollered, "You have to pay for traveling time even if you don't use our labor."

Joe was sticking up for the other movers. "You broke your contract, so you have to pay for it."

"You mind your own business!" Mr. Chiznik yelled at Joe.

"We're all sympathizers when we're in the same business," Chiznik's mover shouted. "If you don't pay us, we'll send some goons after you. I can promise you that!"

Joe's workers, Mario and Gino, carefully lowered the china closet they were carrying. Mario straightened his back and pointed to Mr. Chiznik. "Hey, Mister, you ever have your legs broke? Eh? You play tough with them, they'll play tough with you. "

The three movers slowly strode toward Mr. Chiznik with glaring eyes and tight lips.

"Maybe we'll save the goons the trouble and do it ourselves."

Mr. Chiznik stepped back. The men appeared enormous as their heavy steps advanced on him. They looked like the thugs in gangster movies.

We cheered from the windows, but when I saw them get close to Mr. Chiznik I became frightened. "Mama, don't let them break Mr. Chiznik's legs," I pleaded.

"Don't worry, they won't. They want only to scare him. Watch a minute—Chiznik will give them the money. He may be stingy, but better he likes his legs than his money."

Mr. Chiznik backed up against the moving truck. "All right, all right, don't hurt me. I'll pay you." He took money out of his pocket and glanced up at us from under his brows as we applauded from the windows.

I wondered if, as an adult, Mr. Chiznik could feel as humiliated as I had felt in the school office. His hands were shaking as he counted out the money.

"Aha!" Evy sang out. "He capitulated."

"What's capitulated?" Arnie and I asked.

"He gave up! The coward!"

"Good!" Mama said. She shook her finger out the window. "He's a no-good capitular! " We laughed. Mama pulled us away from the windows. "Come, *kinder*, let's sweep the empty rooms and move already."

Evy grabbed the broom, I took the dust mop, and Arnie picked up the dustpan. I began to sing to the tune of "Roll Out the Barrel."

Roll out the barrel,
The Dormans are moving from here.
Roll out the barrel,
The Dormans, they move every year.

The three of us sang and swept our way out of the house. Mama followed behind, us shaking her head and laughing.

2 Kenubble Trouble

THE THREE OF US AND MAMA SQUEEZED INTO THE CABIN OF THE moving van next to Joe. Arnie held Malkah. The rest of the movers sat in the rear of the truck on the tailgate. None of us minded the tight squeeze; we enjoyed every bump and bounce of the trip.

We arrived at our destination, 610 Maple Street, the first of a row of attached three-story buildings. It was similar to many houses we had lived in before. I knew it would have an inner courtyard. Immediately next to the house was an empty lot that separated it from a small apartment building at the corner. Under this building, angled at the very corner of the block, was a drugstore.

Mama said, "Come, *kinder*, we have a lot of work and not much time. Arnie, hold Malkah close so she won't run away."

He did. He held his white cat so tightly that Joe said, "Hey! The cat is turning blue!" We all laughed.

Joe helped Mama step down from the truck. "Look at that!" I pointed. "I can't believe it! The school is right across the street!"

"Wow!" Evy said. "We could roll out of bed to get on line each morning. Mama, what grade does this school go up to?"

"Only up to eighth. I didn't tell you the school is across the street. I wanted to surprise Leely and Arnie."

Evy and I jumped out from the truck. I grinned with delight. I looked around at all the children playing in the street. Evy looked at the teenage boys playing ball in the schoolyard. She said, "How lucky you are, Leely. You won't have to walk a distance in the rain and snow. I wonder how far the high school is."

"There sure are a lot of kids around here," I said, looking behind me as I followed Mama up the steps. There were kids sitting on the stoop. They stopped talking and looked us over.

Our apartment was one flight up and in the front of the building. We walked through the empty rooms to check it out. There were three bedrooms, the most we had ever had. The smallest bedroom would be Arnie's. It faced the inner courtyard. So did the kitchen and dining room windows. Mama and Papa's bedroom windows faced the street, as did ours.

Evy and I stood at our bedroom window looking out. "I think I'm going to like it here," I said, smiling up at Evy. Evy smiled back but kept looking out to the schoolyard where the boys were.

Mama called to us, "Evy, Leely, the barrels are in the kitchen already. Come empty them so Joe can take them back with him today."

"Hey! What's this?" Arnie asked, looking at a large white box that stood against a kitchen wall.

"It's a refrigerator," Evy said.

"What does it do?"

I opened the door and looked in. "It's instead of our old ice box. It keeps the food cold."

Arnie examined the refrigerator. "What's the funny round thing on top of it? It looks like a giant marshmallow."

Mario, Joe's helper, was in the foyer holding the headboard from Mama and Papa's bed. He pointed to the large round marshmallow thing and said, "That? That's the motor and machinery that makes the box cold. What's the matter, you never seen a 'frigerator before, sonny?"

"No! Never! So we won't need an ice man anymore, Mama?"

"That's right," Mama answered, "no more ice. Now we have two 'lectric 'plientz, this and the press iron."

"Could we have three, Mama? A radio, too?" Evy asked with pleading eyes.

"Yes!" I faced Mama with my hands folded in a prayer position. "Could we pl-e-a-se get a radio?"

"If Papa makes a living in this store." Mama held her arms and eyes up toward the sky. "You hear me, *Gottenyoo*? We'll get a radio. But for now what we'll get is *Shabbas* if we don't hurry and unpack."

The door of our apartment stayed open so the men could bring the furniture in. So did the neighbor's door. There were only two tenants on the floor, and the doors faced each other. In the other apartment a woman turned her armchair so she could see what was going on. Mama smiled and nodded her head. The lady smiled back, keeping her dark eyes steady on everything that went into our apartment: mattresses, dining room chairs, bed linens, towels. Everything!

"Why is she watching us, Mama?" Arnie asked. Mama put her finger to her lips and shook her head.

"Because she's a big *yenta*. A nosy body," I whispered. "She's examining everything we own. It's embarrassing."

"She must be taking inventory of our belongings." Evy commented.

"I guess she feels superior because she has a living room and we don't," I said, thrusting my chin forward.

Mama gave me a poke and put her finger to her lips again. "Sh! Shah! She'll hear you."

We unpacked as fast as we could while the men brought the furniture in. Joe and his helpers placed each piece of furniture exactly where Mama told them. Except for some boxes and dishes, most of the things were in their proper places.

Joe was finished and came in to say goodbye. "Well, as usual, it has been a pleasure to move for you, Mrs. Dorman. Hey, kids! Come say goodbye."

Evy and I went up to him to get our Italian kisses, one on each cheek. Evy said, "See you next year, Joe." Joe chuckled.

"Yeah, see you next year," I repeated.

"God forbid!" Mama yelled from the dining room. "Please, *Gottenyoo*, this should be a good store and my husband should make a living in it for a l-o-n-g time. *Awmein!*"

"Amen!" Joe repeated. "I'm sure you want the door closed now, Mrs. Dorman." Joe gave Mama an understanding wink as he took the last barrel with him.

"*Oy,* please, yes, Joe. Thank you!" Mama ran to lock the door. She leaned her back on it and sighed with relief. "Maybe now we can finish moving in private. *Gottenyoo,* how can a person be so, s-o-o-o big a *yenta?*"

"Brazen," Evy said as she scrubbed the burners of the gas range.

We looked at Evy.

"And what means, brazen?" Mama asked.

"Brazen means shamefully bold. She's a shameful *yenta.*"

Mama nodded her head in agreement. Then she shook her head from side to side. "Tsk, tsk, tsk, such a brazen woman."

We all shook our heads in disbelief, repeating "brazen." Except Arnie; he kept saying "raisin, raisin, raisin."

"Mama, did you see how she let her little baby girl run in the hallway while the men were carrying the furniture up?" I asked.

Evy said, "Yeah, Mario and Gino had to beg her to keep the baby inside so she wouldn't get underfoot."

"Right, and she kept calling her older daughter Rosie to go get her. She never once got out of that living room chair," I added. "Not once!"

"Raisin, raisin, raisin, tsk, tsk, tsk." Arnie kept singing as he shook his head, imitating Mama. He was putting the spoons and forks into the utility drawer that Mama had washed and lined with paper.

It was a small kitchen, and we were working very close to one another. We worked quickly to get the cabinets and refrigerator clean so we could put the dishes and food away before Papa got home.

"You'd think she would close her door and mind her own business," Evy said, still annoyed with the neighbor.

"*Kinder*, you never know who or what your neighbor is like until after you move in. That's why you must always be careful of what you say. It's best to just be polite to your neighbors." When Mama preached to us in Yiddish it was like gems coming from her mouth.

We heard a knock on the door.

"Must be Papa. He's carrying the supper I cooked this morning." Mama opened the door.

There stood our next-door neighbor, smiling. Boldly, she walked into the foyer and looked into the kitchen. We all stared at her. She was big and round like a barrel. Her legs were skinny, and her silk stockings were twisted.

"I'm Mrs. Nemoff. I wonder if maybe I can borrow two *Shabbas* candles. I'm all out." She continued to smile.

Mama looked at me. "Leely, get Mrs. Nemoff two candles." Going to the cabinet, I almost tripped over Mrs. Nemoff's baby. "Oops!" I grabbed the kitchen sink for support.

"*Oy*, Beebe, come here!" Mrs. Nemoff laughed as she pulled her baby away. "She's only eighteen months, and she gets into everything."

Beebe was trying to grab Malkah. Malkah was trying to avoid Beebe and leapt up to the marshmallow on top of the refrigerator. Beebe wasn't cute like other babies. She had crust around her runny nose, dried milk at the sides of her mouth, and hanging wet panties that smelled from urine.

Rosie, who looked about eight years old, stood behind Mrs. Nemoff.

She was skinny, with big eyes and dirty blond hair that needed combing.

Mama introduced herself. "I'm Mrs. Dorman. My husband is the new kosher butcher on the next block, Midwood Street and Albany Avenue."

"Oh! That's you? I'm so glad to hear that. I don't like the butcher up on the hill. He's too expensive and he doesn't give credit. And his meat—" Mrs. Nemoff waved her hand near her ear—"it isn't good either. He's not such a nice person. Phew! The butcher that was in the market before your husband, he died from a heart attack. So we had to go up the hill to Empire Boulevard to buy our meat. *Nu*, so up the hill everything is hotsy-totsy." Mrs. Nemoff flipped her nose upward with her finger and rocked her shoulders from side to side. "And it costs more."

Mrs. Nemoff stretched her neck to look at the end of the foyer behind Mama. "I see you have a dining room, not a living room. Huh! So where do you come from?"

"Mrs. Nemoff, you must excuse me, I have to finish unpacking before *Shabbas*. Maybe some other time we could talk, yes?"

"Of course! Sure! It's nice to meet you. Good luck in your new apartment. Toodle-oo, goodbye." She waved her fingers as she left.

"Thank you, and have a good *Shabbas*, Mrs. Nemoff." Mama closed the door gently behind our new neighbor and locked it. She leaned on the door and sucked in her breath, then blew it out slowly.

"So what do you think, Mama?" I asked with a smirk on my face.

I knew how much Mama hated gossipers and nosy bodies. "Do you think she'll be a good friend?"

"What do I think?" Mama tightened her lips and shook her head. "I think, *kinder*, trouble is what I'm going to have. Smelly trouble, that's what I think."

"*Kenubble* trouble, right, Mama?" I giggled, and they looked at me and waited for an explanation. "Well, *kenubble* means garlic, and garlic smells, doesn't it? So-o-o..."

"*Kenubble* trouble!" we sang together, nodding our heads.

3 New Friends

THE DAY AFTER WE MOVED INTO OUR NEW APARTMENT EVY AND I decided to check out the new neighborhood and the market in which Papa rented a section for his kosher butchershop. We opened our door to leave and looked directly into the Nemoffs' apartment. Their door was wide open again. Squatting on the floor, rolling a ball to the baby, was a girl about my age. As soon as she saw us she jumped up and approached us with a friendly smile.

"Hello! My name is Millie. My mother told me one of you might be my age. I'm twelve years old. How about you?"

Millie's eagerness to be friendly took me by surprise. I was amazed by her resemblance to her mother. She had her mother's round, freckled face as well as her outgoing personality.

"Oh! Yes, that's me! Umm, I'm going to be twelve. I'm Leely."

"And I'm fourteen, going on fifteen." Evy played with her collar. "My name is Evy, but you can call me Dickie."

Millie smiled easily. She looked us over. "What grades are you in?"

"Sixth," I said. Millie turned to Evy.

"Tenth. I made the RA." Evy's nose was beginning to lift. The RA stood for Rapid Advance, where bright students completed the seventh grade in the first six months and the eighth grade in the second six months of the year.

"I'm in seventh. So where are you two going?" Millie asked.

"We were just going to walk around the neighborhood. Get to know where things are," I replied.

"Oh! I could take you around. I'll even introduce you to some other kids on the block. Okay?"

Evy and I looked at each other and shrugged our shoulders. "Sure. Why not?" Millie ran back into her house for her sweater, and I noticed her print dress had an unraveled hem with threads hanging. It looked as though the dress had been lengthened and the hem had never been turned back up again. When she came back out of her house she was smiling pleasantly. "Let's go!"

As we walked down the hallway stairs I could hear voices and the laughter of kids. Outside on the stoop landing I was surprised to see so many boys and girls. They were standing in the doorway, sitting on the sides of the stoop, playing jacks on the steps, and catching a ball in the street. Stunned, Evy and I stood there looking from one face to another.

"Lucky you!" Millie sang out. "The gang's all here! Hey, everybody, these are new kids that moved in yesterday. This is Evy Dorman. She's fourteen, and her sister Leely is twelve."

Everybody stopped talking and looked at Evy and me. I felt as if I were an actress at center stage and they were all waiting for me to speak. Evy must have felt the same way, because she stood there smiling, too, and saying nothing.

Finally Millie started the introductions. "This is Irene, Yussy, Philly, Freddie..."

The tallest fellow interrupted and introduced himself. "I'm Donald Passan. I reside around the corner on Midwood Street. It runs parallel to this one."

That statement caught Evy's attention. I thought I saw her back straighten and her ears perk up. Quickly I announced, "Evy's nickname is Dickie. That's because she loves to study the dictionary." Evy's eyes narrowed as she threw me a "dagger" look.

"Oh! Are you a snobby egghead like Donald?" the boy named Philly asked.

"Not really," Evy answered. "I don't know about Donald, but if necessary, I can socialize with anti-intellectuals also."

"Wow!"

"Hey!"

"Listen to her, will yuh?"

Donald whistled and nodded his head. "Quick and smart!" Most of the kids had a comment to make and not unkind.

The redheaded girl named Irene said, "So you see, guys, we girls are sharp, too, and can stand up to any of your smart-aleck remarks." I soon learned that Irene lived on the first floor directly beneath our apartment.

Everyone made wisecrack remarks and teased. But underneath it all, like a soft plush carpet, there was a friendliness, a camaraderie in the group. They asked us many questions and got to know us. We found out how old they were and which schools they went to. Donald, Freddie and Yussy went to Erasmus High School. Philly Bronson was still in P.S. 91 across the street.

Philly was Yussy's kid brother. They resembled each other a great deal, even though Philly was quite a bit shorter, his hair curlier and blonder, and his eyes much, much bluer. Wow! They sure attracted my attention. I kept looking at them. Never had I seen such a transparent blue. It was like looking through the sky. The boys teased Philly about his size. They called him Peanut. Then they pacified him by telling him that he would grow after he became a bar mitzvah.

I couldn't help noticing that as Philly kidded back and forth with them he squirmed each time they mentioned his height.

When the boys heard that we were going to see where Papa's butcher store was, they offered to walk with us. Of course, Millie joined us.

The market was long and narrow and had two entrances. The front doorway on Albany Avenue was centered between two windows. Papa's section was on the right, the grocery on the left. The rear side entrance was on Midwood Street.

The guys walked us through the front to show us the inside of the market. Since it was Saturday, Papa's section was closed. As usual, Papa had left the store Sabbath-clean when he closed early on Friday. It smelled of fresh sawdust. I felt proud.

"We often hang around the front of the market on Saturday night," Yussy said.

"Yeah, it's bright and lively. A lot of people shop then. And the butcher and Hooney's father don't complain," Donald added.

"Who's Hooney?" Evy asked.

"Mr. Greenberg the grocer's son," Philly answered.

Hooney was behind the grocery counter. The boys waved to him and introduced Evy and me. I was taken aback by his appearance. He had a fat belly, but more surprising were his eyes. Again I was fascinated by eyes. Only his weren't beautiful like Philly's; he had one green eye and one brown eye.

Papa's big delivery bike was leaning against the wooden ice box that separated his butcher shop from the fruit and vegetable section.

"Hey, guys! Take a look at the size of this bike. Wow! Didya ever see one this high?" Philly stopped to examine the bike.

"And look at the size of that metal basket. I've never seen one that large." Yussy placed a hand on each side of the basket as if to measure it.

I sighed. "I know. It's awfully large. That's why I could never learn to ride a bike. Every time I tried, I fell off. It's very heavy."

Philly threw his leg over the bar and tried it for size. "Holy Cow! It must weigh a ton. Nobody could learn to ride on this!"

"Yeah, and the basket is a monster. That's what throws it off balance." The other kids sauntered off toward the rear of the market, leaving Philly and me behind.

Philly said, "You want to learn to ride a bike? I'll teach you."

"Really? You've got a bike?"

"Yeah. And it's brand new! I got it for a bar mitzvah present even though I won't be a bar mitzvah for a few more months."

"Then how come you got it?" I held the bike for Philly to get off.

"My parents said if I studied hard and learned my *Haftarah*—that's the section I have to read in Hebrew—they would give me a bike ahead of time. Then I could ride it before the snows come."

"Gee! So what happens if you don't learn your *Haftarah* well?"

"Are you kidding? They promised they'd take the bike away and I wouldn't get it until I'm fourteen. And when my parents make a promise—they keep it! My parents have a thing about promises. They're always preaching that you're not allowed to break promises, because it's a sin if you do. Boy! Did I go at that *Haftarah*! I practice every single day. It's hard, but I've got it down pretty good. Except for the *trope*, that's really tough. I guess you wouldn't know what the *trope* is."

"Oh, yes, I do! They're those little signs like musical notes so you can chant like a cantor."

Philly's blue eyes got bluer as he stared at me. "How come you know that? You're a girl. You don't become a bar mitzvah."

"Oh, I've been going to Hebrew school for years. I learned how to read Hebrew and to read and write Yiddish."

"No kidding!" Philly kept staring at me. "Okay, what's one of the most important prayers in the Jewish religion?"

"That's easy, the *Shema*."

"Can you say it?" He eyed me sideways and pulled his mouth smugly to one side. I hesitated. "Go ahead. I dare you to say it!"

I closed my eyes and rushed through the prayer so fast I almost bit my tongue. *"Shema Yisrael Adonai Eloheinu Adonai Ehad.* THERE!"

Philly closed his mouth and thought for a moment. Then he asked, "So, do you know what it means?"

"Of course! Hear O Israel, the Lord our God, the Lord is One."

Philly smiled broadly. "So what d'you say? D'you want me to teach you how to ride a bike?"

"Golly! You bet I do! Can we start tomorrow? Gosh, I want to ride a bike so badly, I can't wait."

"Well, tomorrow I have Hebrew school in the morning...and then I have to—oh, never mind that. Yeah, I'll give you a lesson tomorrow afternoon if you want. My bike is so light, you'll learn in no time at all."

"Okay, great! What time?" Delighted, I clapped my hands and stood up on my toes. I dropped down quickly when I realized I was taller than Philly.

"Oh." Philly twirled his hand in a circle as he thought. "After lunch. I'm not sure exactly when, so I'll just call for you when I'm ready. Let me think of a good street to practice on." He opened his eyes wide and looked up. I couldn't get over how blue his eyes were. My eyes were blue, too, but nowhere near as blue as his.

"Winthrop. We'll go to Winthrop Street. It's got a dead end and no traffic, and it's only two blocks away." He smiled shyly and kicked an invisible pebble. "It's a date, then?"

"Sure, okay, it's a date!" I giggled and twisted a long strand of hair.

Philly walked toward the rear of the store. "This is the back part of the market." He pointed his right thumb, "Mr. Schaefer owns the vegetables here. And Frank Alonzo owns the fish store on the back wall. So now you saw your father's new marketplace. Let's get out of here!"

As I followed him through the rear door between the fruit and the fish market I noticed he bounced on the balls of his feet as he walked in his high laced black and white sneakers. I wondered if that was to make him look taller, or cool like the older guys. Outside we found the rest of the kids explaining the neighborhood to Evy and telling her how she could get to Erasmus High School. Donald offered to show Evy where the public library was.

Everyone split to leave. Millie said she would take me to the park. I felt a funny shiver when Philly whispered in my ear, "I'll see you tomorrow."

4 The Bike Lesson

There was a knock on the door. "Come in," Mama called.

"Hi, Mrs. Dorman. Is Leely here?"

From my bedroom I yelled, "Yes, I am, Philly. I'll be right out." I clasped a barrette at the side of my hair to keep my long hair from falling in my face. Evy, who was holding her dictionary against her chest, raised her brows and said, "Look who has a date!"

I lifted my chin and strutted out. She watched but didn't follow. No way was she going to let Philly see her with curlers in her hair. "Good luck!" she said with a smirk on her face.

"Thanks!"

Mama and Philly were talking. "Leely told me your bike is an early bar mitzvah present."

"Yup! That's right!" Philly smiled broadly.

"So when will you become a bar mitzvah?" Mama asked.

"In three months. January sixth."

"*Nu*, you're nervous yet?"

"No, not yet." Philly bent down to pick up Malkah, who was rubbing against his legs.

Mama stopped washing the dishes and faced Philly. "Tell me, Philly, where is the Hebrew school—close or far? I have to bring my little boy to start his Hebrew lessons."

"It's on Albany Avenue, a few doors from the market where your butcher store is."

"It's in a store?" Mama raised her brows. "Not in a synagogue?"

"That's the synagogue!" Philly laughed. "They put a few stores together and made it a synagogue and a Hebrew school both."

"How do you like that?" Mama put her hand on her hip and pouted. "A fancy neighborhood with no big synagogue."

"Mama, I have to take a bike lesson now. We gotta leave."

Philly put Malkah down. "Let's go!"

"Arnie, grab Malkah before she runs out," I said as I opened the door. "Malkah always tries to get out," I said to Philly. "And in this new neighborhood she'd get lost."

"No, she wouldn't," Philly said. "She'd smell you and find her way back."

We heard Mama's muffled voice behind the closed door. "Leely, be careful with the bike!"

Downstairs on the stoop Millie and Irene were playing jacks. We said, "Hi!" Their mouths hung open as they watched me jump onto the top bar of Philly's bike.

"Hey! Where are the two of you going?" Millie asked.

"For a bike lesson," I called back, and I waved goodbye. I could hear Irene say, "So soon?"

The dead end street was short and slightly sloped, which was good for coasting. Only two cars were parked at the lower end of the block.

Philly held the bike while I tried to make myself comfortable on the boy's seat. It was shaped long in the front and kept hitting my inner thighs. Philly's bike was no way as big or heavy as Papa's. Still, I felt just as clumsy.

"Now just let it roll while I push you so you can get the feel of the bike. And don't pedal fast."

"Okay, I won't." I tried controlling the handlebars so the front wheel wouldn't swerve from side to side, but the bike kept tilting. Philly held onto the back of the seat and ran zigzag behind me.

"Leely, hold it straight—straight—S-T-R-A-I-G-H-T!"

"I'm trying, I'm trying, but it doesn't want to go straight. I can't concentrate on everything at one time, Philly. I can't pedal and steer and keep from falling at the same time."

"Okay, we'll try again. You'll get the feel of it soon."

I did try again. And again and again for what seemed forever. I felt self-conscious, clumsy and stupid. Until finally—hurrah—I got the feel. Philly ran behind me, still holding the back of the seat. When he let go I rode down the block, straight and smoothly. "Wheee! It feels wonderful! I love it!"

"Hey, that's good! Real good!" Philly was beaming. "Now we have to work on getting you to start by yourself."

That was not easy. Not with a seat that was much too long for me and a crossbar too high. I was hurting, but I kept right on trying. Nothing was going to stop me now. That is, until I saw Millie and Irene strolling up the street eating charlotte russes. Irene still had the cherry on top of the swirled whipped cream.

"Gee whiz! Who needs an audience?" I said to Philly. "I think I'll call it quits."

"No, you won't! You're just beginning to get the hang of it. You can't quit now."

Getting started had been the toughest part. But I was so determined to ride that I was able to ignore Millie and Irene—even their giggling when I fell and landed on my bottom with my legs twisted around the bike.

Quickly Philly called out, "That's her first flop, so don't laugh. And it won't be her last either."

"Gee, thanks!" I said, raising myself from the ground. "That's not very encouraging, Philly."

"Well, it's true. You gotta fall a lot before you learn. Try again."

"Look who's here!" Millie called out. "Dickie and your kid brother." Evy was, of course, minus her hair curlers.

I felt like a gladiator in an arena. Like in the movies, when everybody came out to witness the kill.

"How come you all knew to come here?" I asked.

"We guessed," Irene said with a chuckle. "It's the only street around here that has no traffic."

I looked at Evy. "How did you know?"

"Yussy, Philly's brother, told me. Just ignore us, Leely. Go ahead and keep learning."

Philly and I walked to the top of the block. "Okay, here I go!" And go I did. Without swerving too much. I controlled my steering beautifully and headed straight down the sloped street. "Yippee!" I shouted.

Suddenly, out of nowhere, there were two bikes riding toward me. On them were Yussy and Donald, no doubt coming to see how the lesson was going. Or maybe to see Evy. Uh-oh! It looked as though they were coming straight at me.

Oh, gosh! I thought. I'm going to go right into them! I panicked. I turned the bike away, but I hadn't practiced turns yet. Nor had I learned how to stop. I swerved and fell, landing in my now-familiar position—bottom down, feet up. Flop number two. I felt my face get red.

Yussy called out. "Did you teach her how to brake?"

"Not yet."

"Well, why not? That's the first thing you have to teach her. If she knows how to stop, she won't fall so much."

Philly placed his hand on his hip and shook his head. "You think you know everything because you're older. Well, that's dumb, Yussy, real dumb. You can't teach the end before you teach the beginning."

"Yes, you can. Just show her how to reverse the pedal. She was riding nicely, but she fell because she didn't know how to brake."

"I'll do it my way, if you don't mind, Yussy. So far Leely is doing fine with my instructions."

I was grateful for their argument. It took the attention off my fall.

"Okay, do it your way." Yussy waved in disgust. Philly continued to teach me—Yussy's way.

"Do it again, Leely. This time when you want to stop, just reverse the pedal."

"Reverse the pedal?" I asked, scratching my head.

"Yeah, just push backwards on the right pedal and the bike will stop. That's the brake," Philly explained.

I was on the bike again. I started by myself and rode straight with full control. I felt as though I had been riding all my life. All the kids were cheering and clapping. "Atta girl, Leely! Hurray! You're doing great!"

Encouraged, I went faster and headed down to the end of the street. As I approached the two parked cars Malkah ran out from between them directly toward me.

"Oh, gosh!" I screamed and turned the bike away. Malkah turned, too, but I hit her anyway.

Philly yelled, "Brake! Reverse the pedal!"

Yussy shouted, "Slowly, don't brake fast!"

Too late. I reversed the pedal so fast that I flew off the bike. The bike slid into the curb. My head smacked into a telephone pole with such force, it sounded like a baseball connecting head-on with a bat. I thought my head had split open.

All the kids came running. "Are you all right?" Evy asked, trying to lift me up. I was shaken and unable to get up or answer. My head throbbed and pounded.

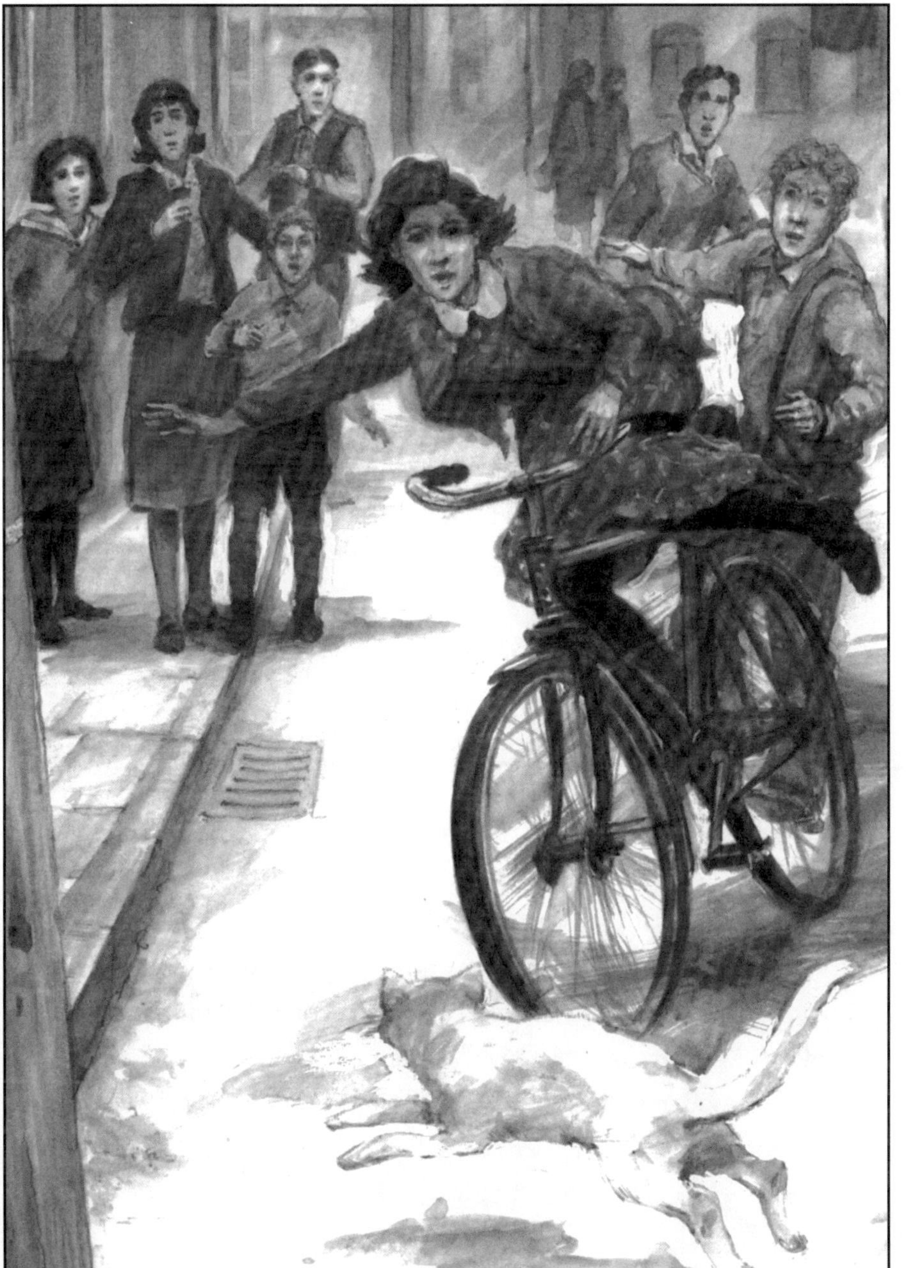

Millie screamed, "Oh, God! Look at her forehead, it's bleeding!"

Evy wiped my forehead with her handkerchief, but it kept on bleeding.

"I-I'm dizzy, but I'm okay—I think."

"Wow! Look at the size of the bump on her forehead. It's getting larger and larger."

Everybody fussed over me. Donald picked me up, Millie brushed my clothes in the back, Irene brushed the front, and Evy continued to dab my forehead. Oh, yes! This was it, the kill they had all come out to see. Only I didn't feel like a winning gladiator; I felt more like a prizefighter who had lost the bout.

Arnie came running. He was crying and screaming, "You hit Malkah, she's dead!"

Jeepers! I had forgotten all about Malkah. We looked at the white cat in Arnie's arms. She was limp.

My heart sank down to my stomach. "Oh, my God!" I bent over Malkah and patted her head. Blood dripped from my brow onto the silver spot on her head. So did my tears as I sobbed. "Oh, gosh! I killed Malkah." Arnie was crying loudly. The kids crowded around him and looked at the dead cat. Nobody spoke.

Then Malkah opened one eye and looked at me. I sucked in a deep breath and straightened myself. For a moment I thought I detected a smile on Malkah's face. Annoyed, I slapped Arnie on the head.

"For goodness sakes, Arnie! You scared the daylights out of me. She's not dead. I only hit her tail. Take her home. Mama will take care of her."

"Maybe she's not dead now, but she was dead. You ran her over and she lost one of her nine lives," Arnie bawled, his tears gushing as he turned to leave.

Donald suddenly called out, "Hey, Philly! Your taillight is broken."

"What?" A quivering cry came from Philly.

"Your taillight, it's broken. Come and see."

"Oh no! Are you sure?" Philly ran up to his bike.

"Look!" Donald had stood the bike upright and was examining it.

"Oh, geez! The taillight's cracked, Yussy. Dad's gonna kill me!"

Yussy checked the rest of the bike for more damage.

"Gosh! Philly, I'm sorry!" I cried. Now everything was going wrong.

Philly walked around in circles pulling on his hair. He kept repeating, "My father's gonna kill me. It's a new bike."

And I kept repeating, "I'm sorry, I'm sorry." Then I heard myself say, "No, he won't, Philly. He won't kill you because I'm gonna buy you a new taillight." I thought to myself, I am? How? And with what? "Umm, how much do they cost?" I asked.

The boys looked at each other and shrugged their shoulders. "I think my brother paid about forty cents for his," Donald said.

"How big was it?" Philly asked.

Donald tilted his head and looked at the taillight. "Smaller than yours."

"Oh, God!" Philly slapped his head. "That's gonna be a lot of money."

"Don't buy it, Philly. I'll get it for you, because I broke it. I'll go home with you and tell that to your father so he won't 'kill' you." I took the handkerchief from Evy and jumped up on the crossbar of the bike that Yussy was holding. "Come on, let's go tell your father."

Philly looked around at everybody. They shrugged their shoulders and said nothing, so Philly and I took off for his house.

Philly approached his father while I stayed behind. "Dad, uh...we had a slight accident and...uh...my taillight is broken."

I blurted out, "It wasn't his fault, Mr. Bronson, it was mine. So I'm gonna buy him a new one."

Mr. Bronson had the same face as Yussy's, only older. He looked at my bleeding and swollen forehead and said, "How slight an accident could it have been if your bike ended up with a broken taillight and this girl with a broken face? What happened?"

Philly and I started to talk at the same time. Mr. Bronson held his hand up. "One at a time, please. I don't understand you."

I rushed to explain. "Philly was teaching me to ride a bike, and I crashed into a telephone pole trying not to hit my cat, Malkah, who got out of the house—I don't know how. Philly taught me really well. I know how to ride now."

Remembering what Philly had told me the day before about his parents and keeping promises, I added, "I promise, Mr. Bronson. I'll get him a new light. And I'll keep my promise, too."

Mr. Bronson stood nodding his head, trying to understand everything that had poured out of my mouth so fast. "That's very nice of you, young lady. Do you have the money for it?"

"I'll earn it. Just give me a little time. I can do it!"

Mr. Bronson threw his hands up. "That's entirely up to Philly."

I looked at Philly, who exhaled a deep breath of relief. "That's okay, Leely, I'll replace it myself."

"No, it's my fault, I owe it to you. Please say it's okay so I can go home. My head is bleeding and hurting."

Mr. Bronson called out, "Sophie! Come take a look at Philly's friend! She needs some medical attention."

A pleasantly plump and pretty woman with blonde wavy hair came into the living room. The whole Bronson family seemed to have blonde wavy hair. "*Oy vey!* Oh, dear! What happened to this girl? Let me look at her forehead." She examined my forehead. "That's some bile! And where else are you hurt?"

"Nowhere else. I'll be fine. I'm going home to take care of it."

"Never mind going home to take care of it. I'll take care of it right here. What happened to you?"

Philly answered, "I was teaching her how to ride a bike."

"Sam, give me a coin. I'll press the bile in."

"No! No! It's okay, Mrs. Bronson, really. My mother will take care of it. Thanks anyway."

The next thing I knew, Philly's father was pressing a half-dollar coin on the bump that Mrs. Bronson called a bile. She held me at the back of my head to keep me from falling backwards while Mr. Bronson pressed. Hard! I bit my lip not to cry out. The pain pierced through my head.

"Push, Sam, push! We can't send her home with such a big bile. Philly, who is this pretty little girl?"

I finally screamed, "Ouch!"

"She's Leely Dorman. Her father is the new butcher at the corner." Mr. Bronson kept pressing, and I felt as though my brains were coming out through the back of my head.

"*Oy vey!* The new butcher's daughter? You pressed enough, Sam. I'll clean it up now. Come!" She pulled me by my arm into the bathroom. Philly followed.

I cried, "My mother can take care of it, Mrs. Bronson. I really have to go home."

"You can't go home like this. What will your mother think if I don't clean you up first? And on my son Philly's bike, yet!" She soaped a cloth and washed my forehead with warm water.

"Philly, hand me the Mercurochrome."

"No!" I screamed. "Mrs. Bronson, please don't put that on my face. Please!"

"Mercurochrome doesn't burn," she said with adult wisdom.

"Yes, it does, and I don't want to go to school with a painted head. Philly, tell her to stop! Tomorrow's my first day at school."

"Mom, don't put it on her if she doesn't want it."

"I don't want her to get an infection." Her voice was firm. I was doomed.

Mr. Bronson came into the bathroom. He looked at me and smiled. "You see, Leely," he said with a chuckle, "my wife always wanted to be a nurse, but since she didn't become a nurse, she practices on children."

"Sam, don't be funny!" SWAB! SPLASH! My forehead was

painted red. I turned to Philly. "If I look like a clown, I think I'll die." Philly tried to control a laugh behind his hand.

"Thank you very much. I'd better go home now." To Philly's father I said, "I'm going to keep my promise, Mr. Bronson, honest I will. I'll get Philly a new taillight." I started for the door. "Thanks for the lesson, Philly."

Mr. Bronson asked, "Philly, did you pick Leely up at her house?"

"Uh-huh."

Mr. Bronson turned his palms out, "So aren't you going to be a gentleman and take her home?"

Philly's face turned red. "Oh, sure, of course I will."

Riding home Philly said, "I don't mind waiting until you save enough money. It's not that the taillight won't reflect—it might reflect better because it has more facets now." We both giggled. My head throbbed with pain, but it also throbbed with ideas on how to earn money.

I walked into the house and slammed the door behind me.

"Who let the cat out? I fell on account of Malkah and nearly killed her and myself."

Evy and Arnie had gotten home before I did. Mama and Papa were awaiting my arrival with wringing hands. One look at me and Mama screamed, "*Gott in himmel!* Look how she's bleeding from the head!"

"God in heaven is right, Mama," Evy said. "He looked after her. She could have been hurt much worse."

"It's not blood, it's Mercurochrome." I started to cry.

"Who put Mercurochrome on you?" Mama asked examining my head.

"Philly's mother, Mrs. Bronson."

Papa's eyes popped open. "Mrs. Bronson, my customer? Nice lady."

Mama looked at Papa and threw her shoulders back. "I don't need someone else's mother taking care of my children. Come, I'll put iodine so you won't get blood poisoning."

"No, Mama, p-l-e-a-s-e! I don't need any more colors on my face. I don't want to go to school tomorrow looking like a clown." Mama carefully examined my wound again and headed for the bathroom.

Papa came over to look, too. He held my face with both his hands. He closed his eyes.

"What? What's the matter, Papa?"

Papa shook his head and talked to me in Yiddish. "I remember when I was hurt on my forehead in Russia. The Cossacks rode through the villages on horses. One of them swung his sword at me. I was lucky. He only sliced off some skin." Papa opened his eyes. He had a faraway look. "Just about the same place where you are hurt." He kissed my bruise and abruptly left the room.

It was hard to know what to say when Papa talked about the Cossacks, the Russian soldiers who had burned Jewish homes and synagogues. They were why he and Mama had left Russia—why I was born in America, not Europe.

After a few moments I turned to Arnie. "Where's Malkah? Is she okay?"

Arnie brought her over for me to see. "She has a broken tail with a bruise on it. " Arnie had put a Band-Aid on the cat's tail.

Mama returned with a three-inch-wide Band-Aid. PLOP! It went across my forehead. The red Mercurochrome snuck out from underneath, and blue discoloration was beginning to peek out from under the red.

Arnie took one look at me and began laughing. With tears running down my cheeks I turned to Evy. "How can I go to school tomorrow looking like this?"

"How?" Evy chuckled. "I'll tell you how. Go to Papa's store. Get the biggest chicken feather you can find. Stick it in the Band-Aid, and go like an American Indian prepared for a powwow. That's how." Arnie rolled on the floor and laughed harder than ever.

I burst out crying. "I'm not going to school tomorrow!" I ran into the bathroom and spent the next hour scrubbing the Mercurochrome off my forehead.

5 Going into Business

Monday morning, our first day of school in P.S. 91, we stood on the stoop in front of our house and looked at the red brick school building across the street. It seemed to have grown taller and darker since I had first seen it. Its windows were like eyes glaring down at me, daring me to enter with my forehead swollen and discolored, looking like a clown.

"I hate going into a new class with this stupid Band-Aid on my forehead. I just know the kids are going to laugh at me." I fought back my tears. "I look so ugly." Arnie stepped in front of me and looked up at my face.

Evy said, "No, they won't. Most of the Mercurochrome is washed off. Don't worry so much about your face. Worry about how you're going to get money for Philly's taillight, now that you promised to replace the broken one."

"I've been thinking about that. I'm gonna ask Papa to let me deliver meat orders after school. I could get tips from the customers."

"Well, that's one way of getting it," Evy said. "Okay, kids, I've gotta get going! Good luck in you new school!"

"You, too." I took Arnie's hand and crossed the street.

"Leely." Arnie tugged at my sleeve. "I think you look pretty. Even with the stupid Band-Aid."

I managed half a smile and squeezed his hand.

We turned to the right and walked around the corner from Maple Street to Albany Avenue, where the main entrance to the school was. The building was four stories high and had wide gray steps in the front. PUBLIC SCHOOL 91 was engraved above the doors. It looked like all the other schools I had been to. Yet this morning, as I walked up the steps holding onto the iron railing, the building seemed as large as a mountain, and I felt as tiny as an ant.

"I bet the principal's office will be smack in the middle of the hallway, just like all our other schools," I said. "I could find it blindfolded."

"Why would you have to be folded if you're blind?" Arnie asked, stretching his short legs from step to step.

"It means with eyes covered." I held the large heavy door open for Arnie to pass through. In the administration office I gave the secretary the manila envelopes with our records in them, and she gave each of us a slip of paper with our classroom numbers and teachers' names. I brought Arnie to his first grade room down the hall and walked up to the third floor to my room.

When I entered the classroom the children were just settling into their seats. The teacher's name was Miss Minsus. She read the admittance slip I handed her and smiled kindly at me. "You look like you've had an accident."

I nodded and forced a smile. "Yes, ma'am." Tears welled in my eyes. Still smiling, Miss Minsus put her arm around my shoulders. "Children, we have a new student in our class. Her name is Leely Dorman. Leely had an accident, and her face is bruised—I'm sure it was very painful. Nevertheless, Leely's face is pretty. Let's welcome her with a warm hello."

The class responded, "Hi, Leely!" They all stared at me, but nobody laughed, for which I was very grateful. I smiled and whispered, "Hi!"

Miss Minsus seated me alphabetically. She handed me a list of books I would need. "The book room is down near the gymnasium, Leely, but I don't suppose you'll be able to find it yourself." She chose a girl from the front row.

"Francy, would you please take Leely for her books?"

Francy sprang up. "Sure!" Smiling, she led me out of the room.

I couldn't take my eyes off Francy. I thought she was the most beautiful girl I had ever seen. She had thick black hair tied back with a rose colored ribbon that matched her dress. Her skin reminded me of peaches and cream, and her large, slightly slanted eyes were a warm brown. She seemed to be smiling even when she wasn't.

I must have been staring at her, because she asked, "What's the matter? Why are you looking at me like that?"

"You're so pretty."

"Oh! Gee, thanks!" Francy's face turned pink. "What happened to your forehead?"

"I fell off a bike and hit my head on a telephone pole. This kid, Philly Bronson, was giving me a riding lesson, and—"

"I know Philly! He lives a few houses away from me. He's cute, isn't he?" I nodded and felt myself blush.

We chatted all the way to the book room and back. She helped me carry my books, and I decided to make her my friend.

Two of the books were the same as I had had in the other school. By the end of the morning session I found I was not behind in any of the subjects. I couldn't wait to tell this to Mama during lunch.

The dismissal bell rang, and Francy and I walked out of the room together. "I have to wait for my kid brother, Carmine. He's only in first grade. I'll see you after lunch, Leely."

"Me, too. I have to meet my brother up at his classroom. He doesn't know his way around the school yet."

I got Arnie and hurried for Papa's store. As we crossed Maple Street I heard someone call my name. I turned. A girl came walking quickly toward me.

"Hey, Leely, I'm Adeline Schaefer. We're in the same class."

"Really? Hi!"

"Your father is the new butcher, isn't he?"

"Yes, how did you know?"

"My father is the fruit man in the same market. Isn't that nice? And we're in the same class, too."

"I'm having lunch at the store. My mother works with my father most days."

"My mother does, too. I have lunch there often, but sometimes I eat upstairs. We live right above the market."

Having just passed Maple Street, I pointed my thumb over my shoulder, "And I live on that block, next to the lot."

As we neared the next corner, Midwood Street, we passed the candy store. "That's Mrs. Jaloza's candy store," Adeline said. "I always get a penny when I finish my lunch. If you can get a penny, we can go to the candy store together."

"Yes, I think I can get a penny."

"First one finished calls for the other, okay?"

"Okay, sure," I answered, happy I was making friends so quickly. I went into the market through the front door. Adeline went in the back entrance.

"*Nu?*" Papa asked. "So how was school the first day? Good?"

"Great! Really great!"

"Is good?" Mama said. "That means nobody laughed at your clown face. And you, *Tatele*, how was by you school the first day?"

"It was okay. I made a friend. His name is Carmine."

I looked at Arnie and wondered if this Carmine was Francy's brother. Then I went to the stove to see what was cooking for lunch. Papa had a single gas burner to singe the tiny feathers off the chickens after he plucked them. Mama used the burner to cook meals when she worked in the store all day. "Mmmmm, vegetable soup."

We ate on the small white table that stood in the corner between the wall and Papa's large wooden walk-in icebox. Mama sat with us and sliced corn bread for us to eat with the soup.

"I like my teacher, Miss Minsus. She's very nice. I knew all the work they were doing. I already learned the arithmetic in the other school. And you know what, Mama? I made two new friends already. One of them is Adeline Schaefer. Her father is the fruit man here in the market."

Mama fixed the brown crescent comb in her hair. "Isn't that something? Already you made two friends in your class. And what is her name, A-de-l-ine? She must be a nice girl, because her parents are very nice."

I took a bite of the cornbread Mama had smothered with butter and pulled on Papa's apron as he passed to go into the icebox. With my mouth full I said, "Papa, can I deliver orders for you?"

Papa stopped to stare at me. "What?"

"Do you have any orders I could deliver for you today—after school?"

Papa thought for a moment. "Why?" he asked.

"I've gotta earn money for Philly's taillight. I promised to buy him a new one, so I thought I could start by delivering orders for you."

"But you can't ride the delivery bike," Papa said.

"I'll walk. I don't care. I have to, Papa. Please!"

Mama and Papa looked at each other for what seemed a long time. They didn't say a word, but their eyes and eyebrows had a big conversation.

"I'll have an order ready for you after school."

I jumped up and gave Papa a big buttery kiss on his smiling lips.

After lunch Papa said I could have a penny. "Me, too?" Arnie asked.

"You, too. You, too," Papa said happily.

I rang up "no sale" on the cash register, took out two pennies, and went to call for Adeline.

"I'm ready, too," she said, wiping her mouth with a napkin. "Mom, Dad, this is Leely, my new friend. I'm taking my penny now, okay, Dad?"

Adeline's dad nodded to her. "So, you're Jacob's daughter. Hello!"

I said, "Hi!" Mrs. Schaefer smiled and put her arm around my shoulder. "Welcome to the neighborhood. It's nice you and Adeline are the same age. I hope you'll be good friends." She patted Arnie on the head. "Isn't he a cutie pie?" Adeline closed the cash register, and we left through the back door.

Arnie held his hand out for his penny. "Gimme my penny, Leely."

Giving Arnie the penny, I said, "You and your mother look so much alike. You both have the same hazel eyes and same color hair."

"Yeah! Rat-colored," Adeline said with a twist of her mouth.

"Rat-colored what?"

"Hair. Rat-colored hair."

"Really? I always thought rats were black." I stopped to look at her hair. "I think it has very nice shades of brown. It's called chestnut brown."

"Ugh! It's awful!" Adeline scrunched her nose and flipped her short hair with a shake of her head. It fell back onto her face.

Arnie skipped to get to the candy store faster. "Arnie, do you think you can cross the street with the rest of the children and come to the store by yourself after school?" I asked him. "It's only one tiny block."

"Yeah, I know how. I'm a big boy!"

"Good!" We reached the candy store, and Arnie ran in first for his candy, a stick of licorice.

At the penny candy counter red-haired Mrs. Jaloza handed me four caramels for my penny. Her hands and nails were dirty. Good thing the caramels were wrapped. Adeline went to the five-cent candies for hers.

"How come you have a nickel?" I asked.

"Sometimes when my parents are busy I take a nickel instead of a penny. They don't know the difference." I bit into my caramel, but I was so stunned I couldn't chew it.

"But isn't that dishonest?" I lisped, the caramel stuck between my teeth.

"What?"

"Asking for a penny but taking a nickel."

"It's not as though it's someone else's money—it's the same family. It's only four cents difference. Here, have a bite." Adeline brought the Baby Ruth up to my mouth. I was about to bite (I loved Baby Ruths), but I turned my head away. I couldn't; I just couldn't. It was as though the candy wasn't kosher.

"I always share." She broke off a piece. "Here, you take this, and I'll take one of your caramels."

I gave her one of my candies and shook my head. "Thanks, maybe next time. I'm full from lunch." We were silent. I felt Adeline look at me from the side of her eye. She probably doesn't feel as guilty if she gives some of the candy away, I figured. Finally I asked, "Adeline, why didn't you just ask your father for a nickel?"

She took her time answering as she chewed. "I guess because he might refuse me. Do you get nickels for candy?"

"No-o-o-o! Never! I wouldn't dare ask for it. My father can't afford to give us nickels for candy."

We walked to the schoolyard in silence.

At three o'clock, when school let out, I rushed to the store. Adeline ran after me. "Hey, Leely, wait up." I waited.

"Why are you in such a hurry?"

"I want to start delivering orders for my father. I have to earn money to replace Philly Bronson's taillight. I broke it yesterday when I fell trying to learn how to ride."

"Oh! Is that how you bruised your face?" Adeline thought for a moment. "You could ask my father, or the grocer, or Frank the fish man, too. They have a delivery boy, but sometimes he comes in late or not at all."

"Really? That's a good idea. Thanks!"

By the time I finished my midday snack of milk and cookies Papa had finished bagging the meat. It was a large bag. "I don't know if you can carry this two blocks, Leely. It may be too heavy for you."

Mama tested its weight by lifting the package up and down with both hands. "Oy! No, Jacob! It's much too heavy for her."

"No, it's not!" I grabbed the package and held it high on my chest. "See, it's easy. Where do I go, Papa?"

"I marked the address on the bag. Mrs. Brodsky, 980 Winthrop Street." Papa pointed in the direction where I had taken my riding lesson.

I walked the two blocks, shifting the package from side to side every few minutes. It seemed to get heavier by the second. *I'd better practice riding Papa's delivery bike, or it'll take too long for me to make these heavy deliveries,* I thought to myself. I was exhausted and out of breath after walking up two flights to Mrs. Brodsky's apartment. Boy! I thought. She must have some large family to need so much meat. I leaned on the door with the bag in front of me while I knocked.

"Who is it?" a woman's voice called.

"Butcher!"

The door opened, and I fell forward smack into a woman's big bosom. "Oy! Who are you? What kind of butcher?" she asked as she pushed me off her and looked me up and down.

"His daughter." I gasped and grabbed the package at my knees before it hit the floor.

"My goodness! You carried it all the way from the market? Wait, I'll give you a tip." She took the bag of meat from me, and I leaned against the wall to catch my breath.

"Oy, it's heavy! You poor dear. It's nice of you to deliver this. Your father must be very busy," she shouted from inside the house.

"He wanted to make sure you got your meat on time."

Mrs. Brodsky returned with two cents. I straightened up to take the tip and knocked over an empty milk bottle that was standing on the floor near the door. People always left their empty bottles there, even if they didn't get special milkman deliveries.

"Would you like me to return this bottle to the grocer for you, Mrs. Brodsky?"

"Bottle? Oh, yes! Thank you! I appreciate it." She bent down and handed me the bottle.

"Thank you, Mrs. Brodsky. My father said you were a very nice lady." I ran all the way back to the store. I was panting, but my face was all smiles.

"*Nu?* How much did she give you?" Papa asked.

"Two cents and a milk bottle. That's a five-cent tip, Papa."

I gave the bottle to Mr. Greenberg, the grocer, and held my hand out for the three-cent deposit. I told Mama and Papa the conversation I had had with Mrs. Brodsky and how I had managed to get the deposit bottle thrown in with the tip. Mama frowned at the bottle part, but Papa laughed, holding his hand to his ear as he always did when he laughed. "Tee, hee, hee. How do you like that? My daughter is going into business!"

I ran home to put the five cents into my *kenippel*, the handkerchief where I saved my money. I untied the knot and put the five cents with six cents I had already saved. Eleven cents. Not bad for a beginning. I'd better find something bigger to save my money in. A knotted handkerchief won't be big enough, I thought to myself. I retied the knot around the money and hid my *kenippel* in the back of my drawer.

6 Mr. Piccolo

SECRETLY, WHEN PAPA WASN'T LOOKING, I TOOK HIS LARGE BIKE with the heavy monster basket and practiced riding. After many painful attempts I finally mastered it.

Beaming with pride, I ran into the store and shouted, "I can deliver more than one order at a time now, Papa. I can ride your bike and go as far as you need me to."

"I know. I know. I watched you steal the bike away and come back riding like a racer."

"You did? You mean it wasn't a secret? You knew all the time?"

"Yup! And I'm proud of you. You ride like a boy."

"Not really, Papa. The seat is too big for me, and I hurt when I sit on it. But don't worry, I can go far. Do you need a delivery?"

"Yes, and it's ready for you. I've been waiting for you to come back with the bike." Papa's pride showed in his smiling eyes as he handed me the brown paper bag. "Take this to Mrs. Piccolo, 911 Midwood Street. Near the end of this block."

Mr. Greenberg, the grocer, hung up the receiver of his phone and turned to me. "Leely, you going out with an order?"

"Yeah, why?"

"I have an emergency delivery. My customer, Mrs. Levine, had an accident and broke her eggs in the middle of baking. Be a good girl, deliver a dozen eggs for me."

"Eggs? Won't they break in the basket?" I asked.

"So be careful. Don't go over bumps or holes," Mr. Greenberg said as he placed twelve eggs into a square egg crate.

"Do you think she'll give me a tip for just a dozen eggs?" I twisted a strand of hair.

Mr. Greenberg looked at me thoughtfully, then shook his finger at me. "Leely Dorman, you're a shrewd little girl. Here's a two-cent tip in advance, but go there first. She's in the middle of baking and must have the eggs right away."

Delighted, I took the eggs, the two cents, and the address. From the side of my eye I could see Papa turn away to hide a smile.

Mrs. Levine had her door open awaiting the delivery of the eggs.

"Hello! Mrs. Levine, are you here?" I called loudly.

A big woman wearing an apron sprinkled with flour and a yellow print bandanna over her hair came running. "So fast? How wonderful." She stopped short when she saw me. "Who are you?"

"I'm Leely Dorman, the butcher's daughter. Mr. Greenberg asked me to deliver the eggs because you need them right away. So I did him and you the favor and brought them immediately. I had to ride very carefully so they wouldn't break."

"Oy, I'm so happy you did. You have no idea how much baking I have to do for my daughter's wedding. Thank you! Wait, I'll get you a tip." She ran back into the house and returned with a nickel. I stared at it in my hand. It was the first time anybody had given me such a large tip in cash.

Mrs. Levine must have misunderstood my expression. "Not enough?" She looked down at the floor. "Here, take these two empty milk bottles also. Now it's better?"

"No, it was fine. Really. Thank you! It's really nice of you."

She smiled. "Take the bottles, too. You deserve it; you did me a big favor. I have to go back to my baking. Good-bye!" BANG! She shut the door.

While riding to deliver the Piccolo order I decided to approach the other merchants and tell them I could make deliveries by bike for them, too. In my excitement I rode fast, pedaling all the way to the Piccolo address in a standing position. The seat was so big, my backside bounced on it each time I turned the pedal.

I rang the bell at the Piccolo house, and to my surprise it was answered by Francy, the pretty girl in my class. Her eyebrows went up when she saw me. "Hi, Leely, how did you know where I lived? Come on in." She threw the door wide open for me to enter.

"I didn't know. I'm just as surprised as you are. I didn't know your mother was my father's customer, and I didn't know your last name was Piccolo." I held the bag toward Francy and entered.

Francy closed the door behind me. "My mother likes that your father is close and delivers. She works and can't take the time to go marketing. I'm making meatballs and spaghetti for dinner."

I noticed the flower print apron Francy was wearing. It looked a lot like the apron I wore when I cooked. "But you're Italian. How come you eat kosher meat?"

"My mother says your father's meat is good quality. She goes to another butcher for pork and bacon. But we're not eating much of that anymore. The doctor told us it's bad for my father." I followed Francy into her kitchen. "He's very sick. He can't work anymore."

"Ah, that's too bad about your father. I cook, too. My mother has to help my father in his store almost every day. If they're too busy and she can't cook in the store, then my sister and I cook at home. But I haven't had to do any cooking the past two weeks because I've been delivering orders for my father. I'm saving the tip money to buy Philly another taillight. I told you how I broke it, didn't I?"

"Yes, you did. I think it was very funny, even if you did hurt your head." She glanced sideways at my forehead. "Which, I see, has healed nicely." She tore open the bag of meat.

Someone coughed in another room. "Come meet my father." She dumped the ground red heap into a bowl and took my hand to lead me into the living room. Francy's father was tall and skinny, with a head of surprisingly white hair. He was sitting in a large club chair next to the window, reading and coughing.

"Papa, this is Leely, the new girl in my class—the one I told you about. Her father is Mama's butcher. Leely delivered the meat, so now I won't have to go for it."

Mr. Piccolo spoke in a heavy Italian accent. "Hello, Leely! Francy, she tell me you a nice girl."

I gave Francy a "thank you" smile. "How do you say your last name? Like the musical instrument?"

"At's right. Just like instrument." Mr. Piccolo smiled, then coughed.

I noticed a piano in the corner of the room. "Oh, gosh! You have a baby grand piano! Who plays that?"

"Both my parents," Francy replied. "They're musicians. My mother was an opera singer, and my father played the flute in the orchestra. He had just come over from Italy when they met. She offered to introduce him to America. They fell in love and got married. Even after my brother and I were born, my mother still sang in the opera. Now she gives me lessons on the piano, and she's going to start teaching my brother."

"The one that's in the first grade?"

"Yes. I only have one brother."

"Same age as my kid brother. I wonder if they're in the same class."

I walked up to the piano and felt the keys. "You're so lucky. I always wanted to learn how to play the piano. Ever since I lived in my Aunt Tzeerel's house in Cleveland, Ohio. I was five years old then, and every time I touched the piano my aunt would make me stop. She'd say, 'You make too much noise.' I never stopped wanting to learn, though." I felt tears well up in my eyes. I wanted to play the piano so badly, I always cried when I spoke about it.

"So why you no play?" Mr. Piccolo asked.

"Oh, because we don't have a piano. We can't afford one. And even if we could, it costs too much to move one. And we move very, very often—almost every year." I sighed deeply.

Mr. Piccolo nodded his head and coughed. "Maybe if you gonna be Francy's friend, we give you lessons, too. Huh?"

My jaw dropped. "You would? You really would?" I looked at Francy. She raised her shoulders and smiled. "I could learn a little bit, even if I have no piano to practice on. Couldn't I?"

"Maybe you'll be able to practice here," Francy said.

"Child"—Mr. Piccolo touched the tips of his fingers together and shook his head—"if you wanna play bad enough, you will find a way."

"Gosh! That's so-o-o nice of you. Thank you very much! As soon as I make enough money to buy Philly's taillight I'm gonna take lessons. Okay?" My eyes were wet again, only this time with happiness. I wiped a tear away and smiled. "I'm a crybaby. I cry over the least little thing." I gave Francy a hug and sang, "Yippee!"

"Papa, we have to give Leely a tip. Do we have any pennies?"

"No! No tip, Francy. You're my friend, and I don't take tips from friends." I ran up to Mr. Piccolo and planted a kiss on his cheek. He smiled and began coughing again. Francy walked with me as I headed out. "Does your mother ever sing in the opera now?"

"No. If you sing in the opera you have to travel with the company. My mother has to be near my father because he's so sick. Now she works in a ribbon factory. But sometimes she gets private jobs singing at weddings and parties."

"Aha! That's why you're always wearing pretty colored ribbons."

"That's right. I have every color I need, and in different widths. Wanna see them?"

"Sure!" I followed her to her bedroom.

Francy kept her ribbons in a basket. They were gorgeous—like a rainbow of every color under the sun. And in widths ranging from a half inch to about six inches. "You're so lucky to have all these ribbons. They're so beautiful." My fingers got lost in the array of satin and silk softness.

Then I jumped up. "Whoops! I gotta go! My father will worry, I've been gone so long."

"I'll walk you to your bike," Francy said. At the foot of the steps she added, "I'm so glad to see you, Leely, I don't usually get friends to come over after school. And I can't go out. I check in with my father at lunchtime and stay home with him in the afternoons. I make sure he takes his medicines and stuff."

"Can you get out on the weekends?"

"Oh, yeah! My mother is home on weekends."

"So suppose we spend Saturday together. Can you have lunch with me?"

"I'll ask my mother. I'm sure she'll say yes."

We reached the bike I had leaned against a tree. "Oh, my goodness!" I cried out, "my two milk bottles are gone! Someone stole my tip!"

"Oh, Leely, that was six cents. That's too bad. You know kids always go around stealing empty bottles and turning them in for three cents. I'm sorry for you." My heart felt as if it had dropped down to my stomach. "Oh, nuts! I was so proud of this tip." I pouted.

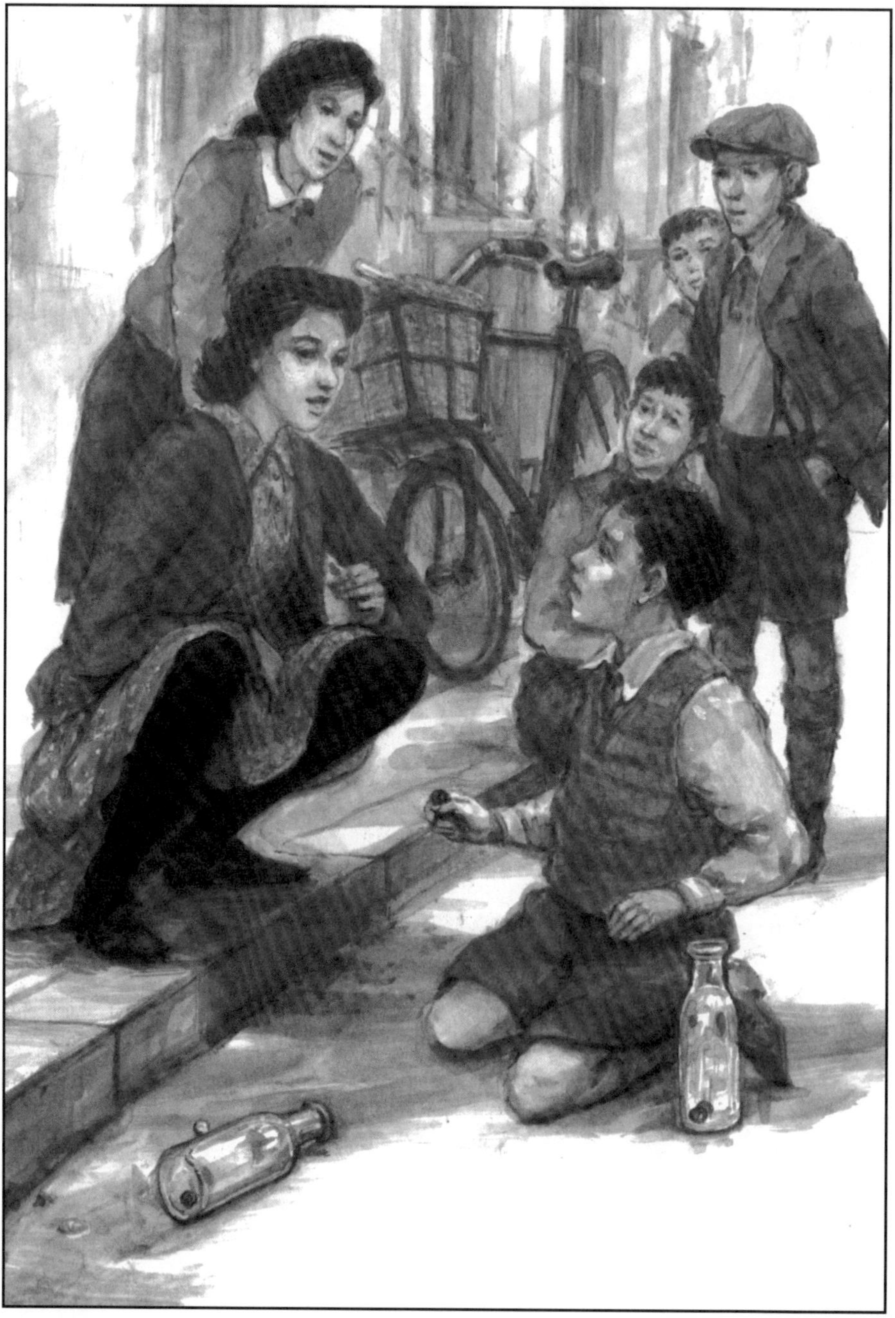

"Carmine, get off the dirt. You're gonna rip your knees. That's my brother playing marbles." Francy's brother and three other kids were kneeling in the dirt alongside the curb. "Look!" Francy pointed. "They're shooting marbles into milk bottles!"

I squatted to talk to them. "Hey, kids, where'd you get the milk bottles?"

Carmine said, "In the bike basket. We borrowed them—we weren't gonna keep them." Carmine was a cute kid. He had curly black hair and dark brown eyes. He looked a lot like Francy. I smiled and tousled his hair.

I stood up and blew my breath out. "Whew! I'm sure glad some kids passing by didn't take them. I'm never gonna leave them out like that again." I returned the bottles to the basket and gave Francy a hug. "I'll see you in school, Francy. Find out about Saturday." I straddled the bike and headed back to the market.

When I arrived I spoke to the other merchants about delivering their orders. Sure enough, Frank, the fish man, had a delivery for me. What a day for earning money! After delivering the fish order I was ready to go home and do my homework. On my way out I met Adeline.

"Hi, Leely, what's up?"

"Adeline, I did so well today. I made fifteen cents."

"No kidding? That's great! How much have you got so far?" Adeline was excited for me.

"I'm not sure. I was just going home to count. Wanna come?"

"Sure, but first let's stop in Mrs. Jaloza's for some candy." Adeline bought another five-cent bar of candy.

When we got to my house I went straight for the *pushka* Mama had given me to keep my money in. It was one of her charity boxes, a blue tin box with a slit on top and an opening in the back to remove the coins. It also had a small hole to hang on a nail. I had scratched my name, L-E-E-L-Y, on the back and hung it on the wall in my bedroom.

Mama hung hers in the kitchen. She made her weekly charity deposits in it each Friday before she lit the Sabbath candles.

Adeline and I laid the coins out on my dresser and counted twenty-nine cents.

"This is great!" I clapped my hands. "It shouldn't take me too long to save enough for the taillight. Even if it should cost fifty or sixty cents. What do you think?"

"I think"—Adeline closed her eyes and bit her lip as she spoke—"I think you'll probably do it in one week if you're going to deliver orders for everyone in the market. Two weeks if you deliver for your father only."

7 Black and Blue All Over

BY THE END OF THE FIRST DAY OF DELIVERING ORDERS ON THE bike my muscles ached all over. Mama said I should soak in a warm bath. I was enjoying just that when Evy walked into the bathroom. She said she had come in to get a Band-Aid from the medicine chest, but she never got it. Instead she stood staring at me with her mouth open.

"What are you staring at?" I asked. She stood there gaping. Then she turned and ran out shouting, "Mama, come quickly, something is wrong with Leely."

Mama came bolting in faster than lightning. She, too, stopped and stared. "*Oy vey!*" she screamed.

"What? What's the matter?" I sat up in the tub and looked around in the water frantically, ready to jump out without knowing why.

Mama screamed again, "What happened to your body?" She stood me up and examined me. I didn't know what she was talking about until I looked down at myself. What I saw was black and blue bruises from my hips to my ankles. Mama turned me around, and screamed some more. "*Gottenyoo*! How did you get so bruised?"

I couldn't see behind me, so Evy described what she saw. "Your buttocks and thighs are completely black. There's hardly a flesh-colored spot anywhere."

I was stunned, but I knew where I had gotten them. "It's nothing, Mama, just bruises from the delivery bike. The seat's too long and big. I hurt when I sit on it, and when I stand and ride the seat bangs into my thighs. It's nothing, really."

"Nothing? What do you mean, it's nothing? You're all different colors!"

Mama turned me around and around to examine me from all sides. Then she pulled on her hair and ran out of the bathroom. "Jacob, you have to stop her!" Her Yiddish words spurted quickly from her mouth. "THIS CHILD IS NOT GOING TO RIDE YOUR BIKE ANYMORE! AND THAT'S FINAL!"

"No, Mama!" I cried, and I grabbed the towel to get out of the tub.

Papa answered in a soft voice. "No, Riva, we can't stop her. She's doing so very well."

"What kind of well? The blood is broken in her skin all over her bottom! You want she should end up in a hospital?"

"Riva, a boy couldn't ride that bike any better than she does. I watched her try again and again. She worked hard to learn by herself. How can we now say no, knowing she suffered all this pain to master that difficult bike? There are times even I have trouble with that clumsy bike."

"*Nu*, that's exactly what I mean. If it's difficult for you to ride, it's worse for Leely." Mama and Papa continued to argue in Yiddish, which they spoke most of the time, and definitely when they were having a serious conversation. When they did speak in English they turned to Evy and me for definitions and translations. We were bilingual and able to help them.

Mama said, "She'll have to find another way to earn her money."

"I'll lower the seat and tilt it so it will fit better for her. The girl has determination," Papa continued, "and I'm proud of her. She's building character, Riva. That's very important."

"Character, shmaracter. I'm not going to let my daughter suffer with pain and bruises and end up in a hospital." Mama's voice softened but remained firm.

I returned the towel to the rack and lowered myself back into the tub, smiling. I soaked up all that Papa had said and I floated with pride. "Building character," I repeated. Hmm, I liked that thought. Yes, that's what I was doing—building character.

I called out, "I love you, Papa!"

"I love you, too, Leely, *mamele*!"

Mamele. Darling daughter. When Mama or Papa called me *mamele*, it felt good.

I sank deeper into the warm water.

Evy returned for the Band-Aid she never had gotten.

"Mama says you're starting a new race of blue and purple people. Don't you hurt all over?" Evy asked as she looked in the medicine chest.

"Yes, I do. But don't tell Mama. I don't mind the pain too much. It's worth having so I could learn to ride that monster bike. But once I get my own girl's bike I won't have bruises."

"Really?" Evy's eyebrows almost reached the curlers in her hair. She wrapped the Band-Aid around a cut on her middle finger. "And just when will you be getting your own bike?"

"When I save for it. After I get Philly's taillight, of course. Then I'll go to work for my bicycle. And I'll get it, too. Just you wait and see."

"What do you want a bike for anyway? I mean, what's so important about having a bike?"

"Look, Dickie," I said as I waved the water, trying to make a lather with the bar of soap, "other than needing it to earn money without becoming bruised, I never really had any toys. No dolls and carriages, doll houses, tea sets, games. All I ever had was a small rubber band ball I made myself, jacks, and a piece of line rope to jump with. The one luxury I would like to have—other than wanting to play the piano, of course—is my own girl's bike. I know we can't afford it, so I'll save enough dollars to buy one. And I won't mind if I get a used one, either."

I kicked the water, splashed waves, and still couldn't work up a bubble bath with the bar of soap. "Anyway, Arnie got his tricycle when he was three, you got your dictionary—I want my bike! But I'll settle for a piano." I chuckled at the impossible thought.

Evy leaned back against the sink and studied me for a while. "None of your girlfriends has a bike."

"Good! Another reason why I want one. It just might be nice to have something no one else has."

"You already have something no one else has."

"Really! What?" I sat up straight in the tub with my hands on my hips. "What've I got that no one else has? Just tell me, what?"

"Aspirations!" Evy counted off on her fingers. "You have aspirations and the perseverance to achieve them." She gave me one big nod and strode out of the bathroom.

Not sure I understood everything she said, I called after her, "Oh yeah? And whatever those things are, can I play with them? And what will it make me, huh?"

Evy shouted back, "An entrepreneur!"

Entrepreneur? I thought. I'll have to look that word up in the dictionary. I don't know if she said good or bad about me.

I stepped out of the tub and dried myself. With the towel draped around me I raised my arm like the Statue of Liberty and marched out of the bathroom singing to the tune of "Yankee Doodle":

> Leely rode a big boy's bike,
> Got banged up to a mu-ush.
> Mama screamed loud when she saw
> Her blue and purple tu-ush.
> Leely Dorman keep it up,
> Leely Dorman dandy,
> She'll start a purple people race,
> If Papa's bike stays handy.

8 Bar Mitzvah Class

I FOUND FRANCY IN THE BUTCHER STORE WHEN I RETURNED FROM delivering an order. "Hi, Francy! Whatcha doing here?"

"I came to pay your father the money my mother owes him."

Papa leaned over the counter and handed Francy a bag of meat. "Here, Francy, here's your meat and here's your change. Tell your mama I said thank you. And also tell her I hope your papa soon gets better."

"Thank you, Mr. Dorman." Francy put the change in her purse, then smiled at me. She looked so pretty when she smiled.

It was good to see Francy unexpectedly. Her brother Carmine was playing with Arnie in front of the store. It turned out they were in the same class. I asked, "How come you were able to leave your father alone?"

"He's taking a nap. He's been very weak lately, you know. He spends a lot of time in bed. Actually, he stays in bed the whole time I'm in school. How are you doing with the taillight money?"

"Pretty good. I have thirty-six cents and this." I held out my hand with two cents in it. "Which will make it thirty-eight. I have to find out how much the taillight will cost."

"Sixty cents."

Francy and I turned to see where the voice came from. Behind the grocery counter Hooney was putting groceries in a box.

"You sure?" I asked.

"Yeah! That's what I paid when mine broke."

"Thanks, Hooney. So I need twenty-two cents more. I can do it in less than two weeks." I turned to Papa. "Papa, do you have any more orders for me?"

"No, *mamele*, that's all I have for today."

Hooney came around from behind the counter. "Leely, if you want, you can have my order. I have groceries to deliver two blocks down Albany Avenue."

"Gee thanks, Hooney, but I don't want your money. You make your own tip." I looked away from Hooney. I had a problem when I spoke to him; I never knew which eye to look at, the brown eye or the green one. So I looked at neither.

"I don't mind. Leely, I'd like to help you." Hooney smiled and lowered his voice near my ear. "This customer buys an awful lot of milk."

Francy got excited. "That's really nice of you, Hooney. Leely, take him up on it. Each bottle is three cents."

The temptation was too great. "Okay. Thank you, Hooney, I'll do it. Is the order ready?"

"Almost." Hooney ran back to complete the order.

"Don't go yet," Papa said. "Mama is in the back of the store. She wants to speak to you."

Francy said, "I call my father Papa, too."

"I know. We must be the only two kids who still call their fathers Papa. All the others call them Dad.

"Hooney," I yelled, "I'll be outside in the front of the store. Let me know when your order is ready."

In front of the market Arnie and Carmine were flipping baseball cards. When Arnie saw me he ran up excitedly. "Guess what, Leely!"

"What?"

"Mama started me in Hebrew school today. And you're going, too."

"*What?* There's no way I'll go. I'm finished with religious school."

"No, you're not!" Arnie put his hands on his hips. "I heard Mama ask the teacher if he had a class for you. So there!"

I turned to Francy. "I don't believe this!" Holding my head with both hands, I spun around. "I can't go to Hebrew school. I have no time for more studying. My mother never stops with this Hebrew lessons stuff."

Francy shrugged her shoulders. "Tell your mother you'd rather take piano lessons. Let's go, Carmine. Papa's alone. We have to go home. So long, Leely, I'll see you in school tomorrow."

Mama came out of the store. "Leely, come with me. We're going to see the Hebrew teacher."

I stamped my foot. "Mama, I'm too old for Hebrew lessons. I've had enough of that. And I haven't got the time anymore. I have orders to deliver, Mama."

"I know that. That's why you're going back to Hebrew school, so you will stop riding the bike. You're bruised all over, and I can't stand to look at you this way."

"Mama, *I don't want to go*! I'd rather take piano lessons."

"Again with the piano lessons. You have no piano to practice on! Forget already the piano lessons."

"I think it's unfair to make me take more Hebrew lessons. They won't even have a class for me."

Mama grabbed me by the arm. "So let's go see if they won't have a class for you."

"Mama, please!" Mama's grip on my arm was strong. In no time I was down the street and in the Hebrew school. The class consisted of eight boys. Philly was one of them. A student was chanting from his book.

Mr. Geller, the teacher, looked up when we entered. He was a short, thin man. I thought he looked like a dried apricot. "Mrs. Dorman," he said in Yiddish, "I told you this is the bar mitzvah class. There are no girls in here."

"*Nu*, listen to how much she knows and find a class for her." Mama pushed me up front. The boys began to snicker. Philly waved his fingers meekly to acknowledge me.

Mr. Geller dropped his shoulders and puffed his cheeks out. He handed me a book, pointed a nicotine-yellow finger (he smelled strongly of cigarettes), and said, "Read!"

One of the boys called out, "Hey, come on, Mr. Geller, no girls allowed in our class!"

Mr. Geller shoved the boy's shoulder. "Quiet!" he ordered. To me he repeated, "Read!"

I read the words easily but didn't chant the *trope*.

The boys started to complain, "No fair. She's not chanting."

I read louder and faster. A red-headed kid shouted, "Aw, she's only a girl, she could never learn the *trope*." I stopped reading. Philly stood up, leaned across his desk, and smacked the red-headed boy on the head with a notebook. "Shut up, Red! You don't know it yourself."

The teacher took the book back and said, "*Nu*, she reads very well, even better than some of the boys. So? So what? Does she know the Ten Commandments?"

Mama stood up straight, thrusting her chest out. "Does she know her Ten Commandments? Of course she knows them!"

"Does she know her holidays?"

Mama's mouth hardened, and her chin swung up. "*I should say so!*"

"*Nu*, so she's educated in Judaism more than the average girl. What else do you want?"

I smiled up at Mama, turned my palms up, and said, "Okay? You're satisfied now? Let's leave!" I wheeled around toward the door.

"Not so fast!" Mama grabbed my coat and pulled me back. "*Nu*, so what if she learns the *trope*?"

"What for, Mama? I'm never gonna use it!"

"Yeah, she doesn't need it." Red backed me up. Philly hit Red on his head with the notebook again.

"Education never hurt anybody," Mama said in Yiddish. "So you'll know how to chant. You'll be able to teach your children."

Philly said, repeatedly nodding his head, "I think you should learn the *trope*, Leely. So what if you're the only girl in the class? Don't worry, I won't let the guys tease you. Right, guys?" They all grumbled.

"Philly, you're not helping me. If I come to this class, I can't deliver orders, and I'll never get enough money to replace your taillight."

"Yeah!" The boys agreed.

"It's okay, I don't care if I wait longer for the taillight." Philly nodded his head quickly, like a woodpecker. "I think you should learn the *trope,* and then you will know everything."

I thought for a moment, then looked up at Mama. "If you want me to be in this class, then I'm entitled to be a bar mitzvah, too."

It became quiet in the room as everybody let the thought sink in. The boys looked at one aother and smiled. Surprisingly, they liked the idea. They stood up, waved their fists, and cheered. "Yeah! Let Leely be a bar mitzvah. Yeah! That's a great idea!"

"Are you *meshugah*, child?" Mama asked. "Are you crazy? You know girls can't become bar mitzvah."

Mr. Geller ran his yellow fingers through his thin hair. "*Oy!* Now she wants to become a bar mitzvah. Mrs. Dorman, do me a favor and let me go on teaching my class. Go see the rabbi. He's in his office. Talk to him about a class for your daughter. I don't have one for her."

Philly called out. "Go ahead, Leely. Talk to the rabbi, but tell him you want to be a bar mitzvah."

The rest of the class agreed and cheered me on. Pleased with the idea, I said, "Come on, Mama, we're gonna see the rabbi."

Mama didn't move. She lowered her voice. "Leely, wait a minute. Maybe we should think about this some more."

"Nope! We don't have to. I like the idea. Come on, we're gonna see the rabbi."

I knocked on the rabbi's door. Mama stood back shaking her head. "Maybe we shouldn't disturb the rabbi."

"Come in."

"Too late, Mama." I smiled and opened the door. I expected the rabbi to have a long white beard, but to my surprise he was young. His beard was short and black, and he had wavy black hair. He smiled at us, and his brown eyes smiled, too. "Come in, come in. What can I do for you?" He spoke in perfect English. The rabbi stood up and put his hand out. "I'm Rabbi Goldstein."

Mama shook his hand. She spoke in Yiddish. "Mrs. Dorman is my name. My husband is the new kosher butcher in the corner market. And this is my daughter, Leely."

The rabbi stretched his hand out to me. It was the first time I had ever shaken hands with a rabbi, or with any teacher, for that matter. I felt important and I liked Rabbi Goldstein right away. He motioned for us to sit.

"Rabbi," Mama began, "I brought Leely in to Mr. Geller's class for Hebrew lessons, but he says he has no class for her. You see, she knows more than the boys, except she doesn't know the *trope*. So now she says she'll take lessons only if she can be a bar mitzvah." Mama slapped her thigh.

Rabbi Goldstein looked at me and laughed. "First we have to clear something up. Do you know what *bar* means, Leely"

I nodded. "Son."

"And daughter?"

"*Bat.*" I felt a light bulb go on in my head. "Oh! Right! I can't be a son of the commandment, I have to be a daughter of the commandment. So a girl would be called a bat mitzvah?"

The rabbi nodded his head and smiled. "Exactly! If there was such a thing. Now tell me, Leely, why do you want to become a bat mitzvah?"

"Well, because I think I learned enough. Mr. Geller thinks so, too. But my mother brought me in here to keep me from delivering orders on my father's bike after school. It's a big heavy bike, and—"

"She's all black and blue, Rabbi," Mama interrupted.

"So," I continued, "if she's gonna force me to learn the *trope*, which is the only thing I don't know, then I might as well do what the rest of the class is doing—become a bar—uh—-bat mitzvah."

"Have you ever heard of any girl becoming a bat mitzvah?"

"No-o-o. But there's always a first time. Right?" I smiled, glancing sideways at the rabbi.

He didn't answer. At least not right away. He rocked in his swivel chair and looked at me.

The door opened, and Mr. Geller stuck his head in. "She reads very well, Rabbi, even better than any of the boys." And he disappeared behind the door.

The rabbi leaned all the way back in his swivel chair. I thought he would fall backwards. He rolled a pencil in his hands and kept looking at me. I could see he was deep in thought. He kept rocking, and thinking, and looking at me. A clock on his desk ticked. It felt like hours instead of seconds.

"You know, Leely, this is a conservative synagogue. Here women do not go up to the Torah. The congregation would be outraged if you walked onto the *bimah*."

"Why? Is there a law that says we can't?"

"No. But it just isn't done."

"Is there a law that says I can't study as much as a boy?"

"No." The rabbi laughed. "There isn't such a law. A girl can study as much as a boy or more, but they have never permitted a woman to read from the Torah."

"Why not? I know the orthodox Jews don't allow the women to sit with the men, but the conservative Jews do. They're more modernized, aren't they? So maybe they can be more modernized with bat mitzvahs, too."

The rabbi covered his mouth and beard with his hand, but I could tell by his eyes he was smiling. He kept rocking in his chair and saying nothing as he studied me. Then he looked at Mama, who sat with crossed arms, taking it all in. She, too, was trying to hide a smile.

"Rabbi Goldstein, you don't know who you're dealing with here. The reason I brought Leely in to learn more is to keep her off the bike.

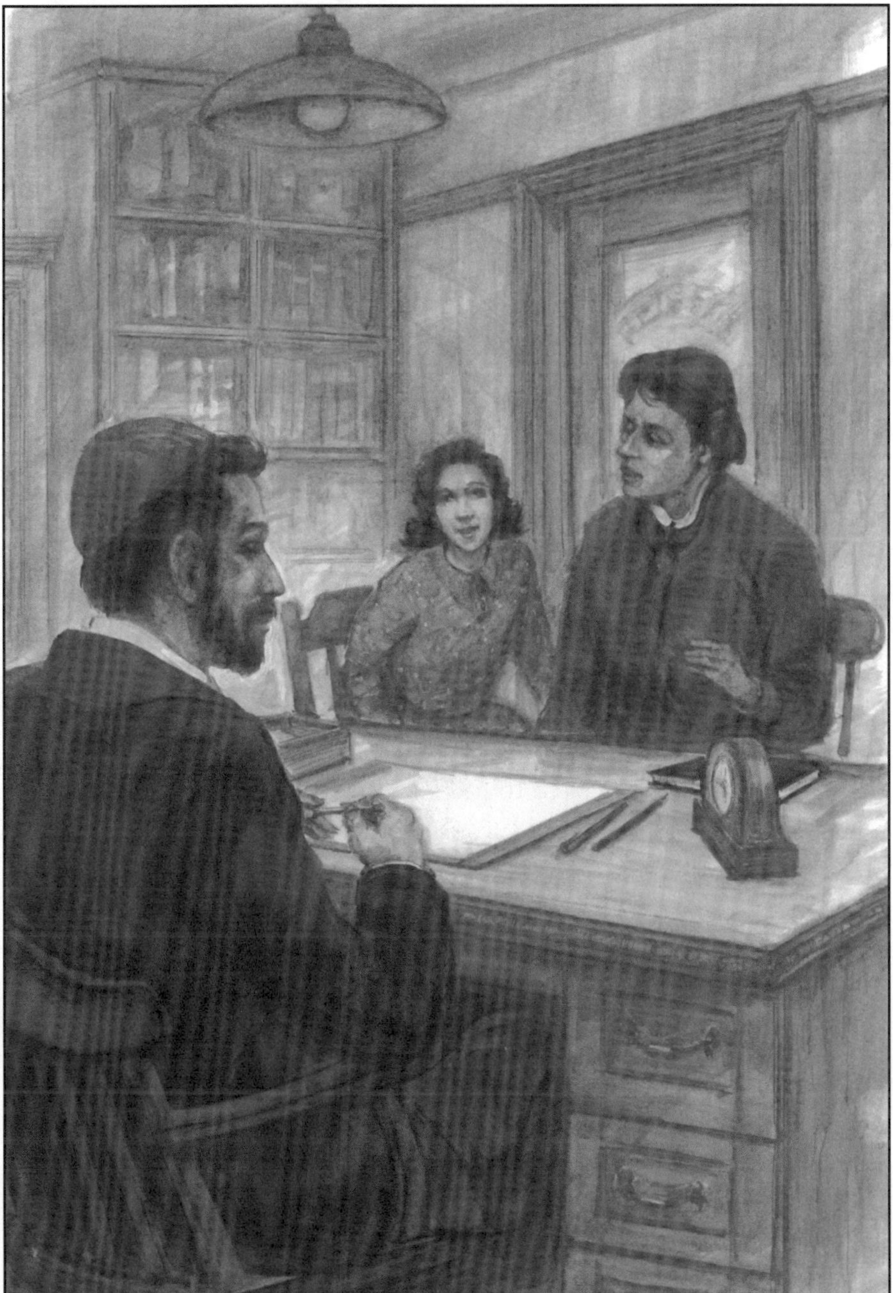

She went into business delivering orders. Now—unheard of—she wants to be a bat—what? A bat mitzvah? Who knows? This girl will be the first woman president of the United States. She always dreams up something new to do."

"You know, Mrs. Dorman, it isn't exactly unheard of. Reform Jews have been having bat mitzvahs for about ten years now. And it's very possible that some conservative synagogues may have already started to do the same. But our synagogue is a bit behind the times. I don't know if they'll go along with it. However, Leely, I will talk to the board of directors and the religious committee and see if I can convince them to accept the idea.

"Right now, let me hear you read." He handed me a prayerbook.

"Where should I read?"

"Anywhere."

I read one paragraph and the rabbi said, "That's enough. Do you know your holidays and Jewish history?"

"I think I do." I looked to Mama. "I can also speak basic Hebrew words and sentences."

"Rabbi, Leely's been going to Hebrew and Yiddish school for over six years already."

"Well, if the committees go along with this new idea of bat mitzvahs, I'll have a session with Leely, and I'll find out exactly how much she knows. Until then I guess she'll have to get black and blue from the bike. Why do you need to have money, Leely?"

I took a deep breath. "I broke the taillight on Philly's bike while he was teaching me to ride, and I promised him and his father that I would replace it. And I must keep my promise. I need twenty-two cents more."

"So, Mrs. Dorman, can't you help her out with the rest of the money so she won't have to ride the bike?"

"Yes, I can, but her father won't. Don't ask what I have with him! He says that it's her responsibility. He says that she's building character."

"I can see that, all right." The rabbi stood up and walked us to the door. "I wish you luck with your deliveries, Leely. I'll get in touch with you as soon as I have information for you."

Outside it had begun to rain. Luckily we were close by Papa's store, and we ran there. I was too late for the grocery delivery. Hooney had already made it. I sat down at the white enamel table to do my homework.

My eyes kept wandering to the rain. I thought of what it would be like to be the first girl in the neighborhood to become a bat mitzvah. Afterwards, maybe other girls would want to do the same. That would be great. The more I thought of it, the more I liked the idea.

9 Murder and Dead

THE RAIN AND WIND BEAT HARD ON THE WINDOWS SUNDAY afternoon. Evy and I were reading on our beds, and Malkah sat on the sill, fascinated with the action on the windowpane. It sounded like pebbles hitting the glass. I couldn't concentrate. My mind wandered as I stared at the running patterns of raindrops on the window.

"Evy, know what I think?"

"What?"

"I think it's time to modernize our parents."

Evy looked at me as though she was giving this some thought. "Do you really? And how do you intend to do that?"

"First, by calling them Mother and Dad. What do you think?"

"I agree with you. None of my friends call their parents Mama and Papa. Only how do you modernize immigrant parents who speak with a heavy Yiddish accent?"

"By telling them that's what we would like to call them." I sat up at the edge of the bed. "Now!"

"Now?"

"Sure! They're both home. It's as good a time as any, if not better." I jumped off the bed.

"Okay with me." Evy looked down at her dictionary. "Just let me finish reading the definition of this word."

I sat back on my heels and waited. "What's the word?" I asked.

Evy read slowly, moving her finger under each letter. "'Trans-mog-ri-fy,' to transform or change completely—"

"Good word!" I interrupted. "Let's go trans-mog-ri-fy Mama and Papa into Americanized parents."

"No, dummy! You can't. I'm not finished with the definition." She read on. "'Especially in a grotesque or strange manner.' That means they could change into an ape, or a cat, or something ugly."

"Ugh." I flipped my hand into the air. "Then we'll just transform them from Russian immigrants to modern American parents. Let's go!"

Malkah leapt from the windowsill to the bed and stared up at me for her next move. I picked her up and called to Arnie, who was playing on the floor in his room. "Come on, Arnie, we're going to do some transforming."

He jumped up. "What's tra-a-nsfor-ming?"

"We're going to change Mama and Papa's names," Evy answered.

"But I like their names—Riva and Jacob. I even like Dorman. They're nice names." He took Malkah out of my hands and sat himself down on the kitchen floor. Papa's wavy black hair was buried behind the Jewish newspaper, and he was reading out loud to Mama. She stood at the gas range waiting for the teakettle to boil.

Evy and I cleared our throats. Papa's bulging blue eyes looked up, and Mama's soft gray eyes smiled at us. They both waited. I pointed to Evy. "You start."

"Umm—Leely and I would like to do a little modernizing in this house. We would like to change how we address you." Mama scrunched her face up like an old apple and looked at Papa. Papa shook his head. He didn't understand either.

He said, "All of a sudden you want to dress us? We can't dress ourselves anymore?"

I got right to the point. "We would like to call you Dad. All our friends call their fathers, Dad."

Papa's eyes popped. "You want to call me *dead*?" His and Mama's accents prevented them from pronouncing vowels and consonants properly.

"Da-a-a-d," we corrected him together.

"I heard you, Deh-he-d," Papa repeated.

"And me? What would you like to make me modern with?" Mama asked.

"Mother," I answered.

"*Murdder?*" Mama echoed. "*Nu*, hello, America! Very nice. Very nice. You want to murdder me and make Papa dead. And that you call what? Mo-derr-nizing? Phew! If you don't mind, I'll stay old-fashioned, but alive."

Evy and I burst out laughing. Arnie giggled and rolled on the floor.

"No, Mama, I didn't say murder, I said mother. Mo-*th*-er."

"*Nu*, I said, mur-dd-er."

"No, Mama." Put your tongue between your teeth like this, Evy demonstrated. "Mo-*thhh*-er."

Mama put her tongue between her teeth and slipped it right back into her mouth. "Murdderrr."

Evy threw her hands up, but I didn't give up. "Okay, we'll make it easier for you. We'll call you Mom for the time being." I looked at Evy for agreement. She nodded her head and shrugged her shoulders at the same time. "But we still want to call Papa Dad."

"No!"

"No what?" I asked.

"No! I don't want to be called dead! I'm not dead yet. I'm alive, and I'm going to be alive for a long time." I knew Papa meant to be funny, but he was serious, too.

Arnie laughed and continued rolling on the floor with his legs up. Evy and I looked at each other and raised our shoulders.

"Okay," Evy said, "I've got the solution. We'll call you Daddy until you get used to the change. How's that?"

Papa looked at Mama. "Riva, you like this modern name, Dedy? Looks like if in America you want to live, you have to become muddered and dead first."

"*Nu*, if you want us to mo-derr-nize," Mama said, "we'll mo-derr-nize, but you must still give us old-fashioned respect. You hear?

Mo-derr-nize, shmoderrnize," Mama said to the teakettle as she removed it from the burner.

"We hear," the three of us answered. We hugged and kissed them both and strolled back to our bedroom. Arnie marched behind us swinging Malkah above his head and repeating, "Murder and dead, dead and murder, murder and dead."

Evy lay down on the bed with her arms folded behind her head. I sat on the bed cross-legged, satisfied with the results of our first attempt to modernize our parents.

"That wasn't too hard," I commented.

"Uh-huh. Now all we have to do is remember to call them by their new names." Evy giggled. She was staring at the wall. "Leely, where's your *pushka* with the bike money?"

I looked up at the spot where I had hung the blue charity box. The nail was there, but the box was gone. "Gee! I didn't even notice it was missing." I jumped off the bed and looked on the dresser. "It must have dropped to the floor." I looked on the floor.

"Leely, the nail is still on the wall. If it fell off, the nail would fall with it. It had to be taken off."

"Maybe Mama put it into my drawer." I opened the drawers and looked through all the folded clothes. Evy got up to help me look.

"I know," I said, "I bet Arnie took it off. Arnie! Come in here!" Arnie came in, rattling his marbles in a jar.

"Arnie, did you take my *pushka* off the wall?"

"No. What's a *pushka*?"

"My little blue money bank."

"I didn't know you had a *pushka* bank. Where was it? I wanna see."

"Up here." I pointed to the nail on the wall. "It was up here."

"Nope, I can't reach that high."

My heartbeat picked up speed. I ran into the kitchen. "Mama, do you have my *pushka* with the bike money?" Already I had forgotten to use her new name.

"No. Why?" she asked.

"It's missing!"

"Why should it be missing? Who would take it?" She looked at Papa.

Papa said, "Don't worry, it's not missing, it's not missing. Look on the floor, maybe it fell down."

"It didn't fall down because the nail is still on the wall. And I looked in my dresser drawers and on the floor. It's not there!" I felt the beginning of tears well in my eyes.

Mama and Papa got up. "We'll look, we'll find it." Mama said. "Don't worry, it didn't get lost."

In the bedroom Arnie and Evy were on their knees looking under the beds. "It's not under here," Evy said.

Papa pushed the dresser away from the wall; Mama looked in the closet. She checked the drawers again and looked in the corners of the room. Then she sat on my bed to think.

"Leely," Papa asked, "who do you bring into your room? Do your friends come in here?"

"Sure." My voice cracked. "My friends always come into my bedroom."

"Do they know you have a *pushka?*" Mama asked.

"Of course they know. They all know I'm saving for Philly's taillight. In fact, Adeline helped me count my money again just the other day. I had forty-three cents, almost enough for the light." I burst out crying.

"And they all know you keep it on the wall?" Mama asked.

"I guess so. How can they miss seeing it?" I sobbed.

"Let's keep looking all over the house. Maybe it will show up," Papa said as he looked behind the radiator. Everybody searched the apartment behind doors, chests, drawers, closets, but there was no *pushka*.

I walked in circles with my hands on my head, crying louder and louder, "Oh, my God! I'll have to start all over again. It'll take me forever to replace the light. How am I gonna explain to Philly why it's taking me so long? And which one of my friends would dare to take the *pushka?*" I stopped walking in circles and thought for a moment.

"Oh, no!" I cried out. My hand flew to my mouth. Mama looked at me. I looked at Mama and sobbed behind my hand. Mama took me in her arms. "Leely, *mamele*, I know how important this money is to you, and how hard you worked for it. Papa and I are very proud of you. If somebody took it, there is nothing you can do about it. You can't accuse anybody because you didn't see them take the money." Mama kissed me on the forehead and held me close. I cried that much harder.

"You'll start again, and you will save even faster this time. You'll see, you can do it! If anybody can do it, you can! And the thief will have to live with her conscience."

I wept harder and walked with Mama's arm around me into the dining room. "I have to start from scratch," I cried. "I don't even have one penny."

Papa brought me a little suede pouch he used for his watch. "Here, *mamele*, put your money in here from now on, and keep it in the back of your drawer so nobody will be tempted."

I wiped my wet face with the back of my hand and took the pouch.

There was a coin in it. I looked up at Papa. He was smiling. "I put ten cents in for good luck, so this time it will grow faster." I gave Papa a blubbering wet kiss and returned to my bedroom. I sat at the edge of my bed looking at the pouch and sniffling.

Evy put her arm around me. "I empathize with you, Leely. I feel hurt and disappointed, too." She sighed and shook her head. "I can't imagine why any one of your friends would want to steal this hard-earned money, knowing how important this is to you."

"Well, I can imagine not only who, but why. Mama says I can't say because I didn't see her do it." I went back to crying.

Evy said, "You don't have to I can guess. Does she have a sweet tooth?"

Arnie came in and stood directly in front of me. He held his hand out. "Here, Leely, take my penny."

This started me crying again. "Arnie, I don't want to take your penny. You save it."

"I want to help you, too!" Arnie pouted.

Evy stood up and went for her purse. "This is a family affair, Leely.

We have to help each other." She took a nickel out of her bag and gave it to me. "It's all I have." She sat down next to me. "But at least you can start off again with sixteen cents."

"Thank you! Thank you both!" I kissed Evy on the cheek and planted a kiss on Arnie's nose. He climbed into my lap and put his arms around my neck. "Don't cry anymore, Leely." He wiped my tears with his little hand. "You're gonna save so fast, it'll be like magic. You'll see."

"I'll have to do more than just deliver orders. It'll take too long to save the rest. I have to think of something else." We all thought silently.

Arnie said, "You could wait in the drugstore for the phones to ring and run to call people to the phone. They'll give you a tip."

Evy's face lit up, and I sat up straight. "That's a great idea, Arnie! I guess I could do that on Saturday nights and Sundays."

"Also," Evy added, "you could babysit. If you do as much as you can, you'll get the money that much sooner, and you'll be finished with it. And I for one, will be very happy for you!"

I looked out the window. The rain dwindled down to a drizzle. "Look, it's not raining anymore. I'm gonna start now." I grabbed my coat and a book to read. In no time I was waiting by the phones at the drugstore.

10 Middle C

I WORKED HARD TO REPLACE THE *PUSHKA* MONEY THAT HAD BEEN stolen from the wall. On weekends or after school, if there were no orders for me to deliver, I would wait in the drugstore for phone calls. Not to waste precious time, I would do my homework in between calls. My friends were very considerate; they kept me company while I was working.

This time Irene and Millie were with me. We were jumping rope in front of the drugstore when Adeline came looking for us. She was eating a jelly apple. Adeline was always eating something delicious, and I knew only too well how she got it. If it wasn't money she swiped from her father's cash register, it was probably from my *pushka*.

"Hi, girls!" she said, her teeth chomping on the hard jelly.

"Hi, Adeline!" we answered.

"Leely, why don't you call for me anymore? I always have to come looking for you. You know I'll stay with you wherever you're working, here or in the market."

I bit my lip and looked down at my shoes. "Umm...it's because umm...I never know where I'll be working for tips."

"Want to jump rope?" Millie asked.

"Uh-huh" was all Adeline could answer with her mouth full. She pointed to her jelly apple until she swallowed. "Just let me finish my jelly apple; then I'll play. Anyone want a bite?" She held out her apple. Millie and Irene took bites.

I said, "No, thanks." It wasn't that I didn't like jelly apples. I did. And I would have loved to bite through the hard, sweet, crisp red jelly to the juicy white apple underneath. I just couldn't. In my heart I felt that it was my hard-earned tip money that bought this jelly apple for Adeline. It was really *my* apple. I should take a very *big* bite.

On second thought I said, "Okay, I will." And I did just that. I took a very big bite.

We jumped rope until the phone rang. I dashed in and out of the drugstore to deliver a message to Mrs. Bloom, three houses away. When I returned. the girls asked, "How much?"

"Two cents."

"How much do you have now?" Irene asked.

"Twenty-three cents."

She let out a deep breath. "Well, when you save up the full amount we'll all celebrate." My friends all knew about the missing *pushka*. That's why they were there—to be supportive.

"Yeah, we'll go to the bike store with you and help you pick the nicest taillight they have," Adeline added.

I laughed. "That'll be fun. All my friends piling into the store with me to pick one little taillight." To myself I said, No way she coming with me to buy the taillight. No way!

The phone rang again. This time I didn't dash out. I walked out smiling. "Would you believe? It was your father, Adeline. He said he and the fish man have orders for me to deliver. My father told him where I was, and your father looked up the drugstore number. How about that?"

"We'll stay here," Millie said, "and if a call comes in, I'll get it for you and give you the tip."

"No, Millie, I appreciate your kindness, but I don't think it's fair to you."

"I don't mind at all, Leely, honest. I want to be helpful. That's what friends are for!"

"Thanks, Millie, but I don't feel comfortable taking what belongs to you."

"Then we'll walk to the market with you and jump rope there until you come back," said Adeline.

The fruits and vegetables and fish were all going to the same customer. Just as I was getting on the bike to leave Papa rapped on the store window. I turned around, "Dad, do you want me?" Papa was at the long end of the counter. He didn't answer.

"Dad...Dad...Daddy..." No answer. I blew my cheeks out. Obviously Papa didn't remember he had a new name. "Papa, did you want me?"

"Yes, Leely, I have Francy's meat ready. You can take it with you."

"Papa, when I call 'Dad' I mean you. Please try to get used to it, because that's your new name."

"So okay, I'm Dead. If I live long enough, maybe I'll remember to be Dead."

"Well, at least try to remember." I walked out of the store with the package. "Girls, you gonna wait for me?"

"We'll wait," they said together.

With another three cents in my pocket from the fish and vegetable delivery I rode to Francy's house with her meat. I found her outside stooping under a tree. "Hi, Francy, what're you doing?"

"Gathering autumn leaves."

I stepped off the bike onto piles of dry, crunchy leaves. "Some of them have beautiful colors, haven't they?"

"Oh, yes! Come see the pretty ones I found." We sat on the steps of Francy's house where she had neatly piled some colorful leaves.

I held up a deep red leaf, "Look at this one. It's the color of wine."

"And this one is purple, like grape juice," Francy said.

"Wow! This one is tomato juice—it's a bright red. What are you going to do with them?" I asked.

"They're for my father. He loves nature with all its colors. He always says the world is full of beauty, but people are too busy to stop and notice it. I'll decorate the dinner table with them. He'll love it."

I looked at Francy and felt a swelling inside my chest. "Francy, have you noticed that when we're together we don't just play games like the other girls do? We talk about different things, like nature and piano lessons, and feelings. I don't talk about those things with the other girls."

"Of course I've noticed. That's why I look forward to the weekends with you. We share a lot. Right?"

Then I had a thought. "You know what, Francy?"

"No, what?"

"Saturday let's go to the park. If you can find such beautiful colored leaves from just one tree, imagine what we can find from all the different kinds of trees in the park. They'll be absolutely breathtaking. Right?"

"Absolutely right! But don't you want to work telephone calls?"

"I don't do telephone calls in the daytime on the Sabbath. I do them in the evening. That's when most of the calls come in anyway."

"Then, super! Let's go to the park on Saturday."

"You'd better bring the meat in, Francy. I'll come, too, and say hello to your father."

Mr. Piccolo greeted me with a strong smile but a feeble voice. It seemed to me he was weaker each time I saw him. Francy spent more and more time with him. Mrs. Piccolo was never home during the day. I only saw her on weekends.

"Hello, Leely! How you are?"

"Good, Mr. Piccolo, how about you?"

"Aah!" He waved his hand from side to side. "The world is beautiful, but I am too sick to enjoy."

"You don't have to go out to enjoy it, Papa. I brought the beautiful world to you. Look!" Francy held the leaves out to her father.

"Ah, Francy, you're a good daughter. You got a beautiful heart. Beautiful like the leaves. Warm like the colors." He took Francy into his arms and held her close. Then he kissed her on each cheek.

"Mr. Piccolo, we're going to the park Saturday. We can gather different kinds of leaves for you, if you like."

"That's nice, Leely. I like that."

The lid of the piano was open. I walked up to it. Remembering my Aunt Tzeerel always complained that I made too much noise, I gently ran my fingers across the ivory keys, making no sound at all. But my heart made sounds. I could hear it thump. I wanted so much to play the piano.

Mr. Piccolo watched me. "So, Leely, when I gonna give you a piano lesson, huh?"

"Gosh, Mr. Piccolo, I can't wait. Soon. I'll be finished saving for the taillight real soon. Then I'll concentrate on the piano lessons." My finger touched one of the keys.

"You know name of key you touch?"

"No."

Holding onto the piano, Mr. Piccolo lowered himself slowly to the edge of the piano bench and motioned for me to do the same. "I gonna give you first lesson. Where on keyboard is the key you touch?"

"In the middle."

"Yes! It is called middle C. Most important key."

My eyes opened wide. I was anxious to learn whatever I could. "Really? Why?"

Francy jumped in with the answer. "Because it separates the treble staff on the right from the bass staff on the left." She swayed her hands gracefully from middle C to the right, then from middle C to the left.

I looked at Francy and her father and smiled. "That's easy to understand."

"Good! You know what is staff?"

"Oh, yes! We learned that in music class. But I only know the staff with the treble clef. E G B D F are the lines, and F A C E are the spaces."

"'At's good! Now press middle C with your thumb."

I pressed and said, "Middle C." Quickly I pulled my hand away and brought it to my chest.

"What's matter?" Mr. Piccolo asked, frowning.

"I felt a shock from the key. It went from my finger through my arm to my heart."

"No, no, Leely." Mr. Piccolo laughed. "That's excitement. Is from your heart to your hand. Not from key, but from your heart. Understand? Yes?"

"I guess you're right, Mr. Piccolo, because my heart is beating very fast." I played middle C again with my thumb. I placed my forefinger on the key next to it and looked at Mr. Piccolo. "D?"

He nodded. "Yes."

I moved my middle finger to E, and before I could play the next key he tucked my thumb under my hand and placed it on the F. I went up the keyboard playing and saying each note. Mr. Piccolo kept turning my thumb under when necessary until I finished playing all the keys on the treble side of the piano.

I smiled broadly, enjoying the accomplishment. "What are the black notes?" Mr. Piccolo laughed and coughed.

Francy said, "They're the flats and sharps, which you're not ready to learn yet."

Mr. Piccolo raised one finger. "First lesson. No hurry. You practice same next time you come, then we do left hand."

I clasped my hands to my chest. "My first piano lesson!" I pressed my hands tighter together. "My first piano lesson," I repeated in a whisper.

I turned quickly and hugged Mr. Piccolo with all my might, forgetting his lung sickness. "Thank you! Thank you! You made me very happy." I must have hugged him too hard; it brought on a coughing spell. He nodded his head but continued to cough. Francy ran to fetch some water. It eased his cough, but not completely.

"Does he need his medicine?" I clenched my fists and bit my lip.

"Is all right. No worry." Mr. Piccolo gasped in between coughs.

"I'm sorry, Mr. Piccolo, I didn't mean to make you cough."

"No worry." He waved me on.

I walked to the door of the living room and turned to look at Mr. Piccolo again. Francy had taken him to his chair and was giving him a spoonful of medicine. She waited until his cough subsided and he was able to catch his breath.

"I'm sorry, Francy, it was my fault."

Francy walked with me to the door. "No, it wasn't. He gets those coughing spells often." She opened the door. "I'll see you in school tomorrow. Oh! I almost forgot! My next-door neighbor, Mrs. Garcia, is looking for a babysitter for her two-year-old son so she can go to the beauty parlor. I told her about you, and she said she'd pay you ten cents an hour."

"Ten cents an hour? That's fantastic! How many hours does it take in the beauty parlor?"

"I don't know. Let's go ask her. But let me check my father first." Francy ran back. "You okay, Papa? You sure? Okay, I'm going next door to Mrs. Garcia for two minutes. I'll be right back."

Mrs. Garcia was young and sort of plain-looking. She had a thin face with olive-colored skin. Her hair was brown, and she had blue eyes. She was very pleasant. "Hello, Leely! Francy told me you'd make a good babysitter. You wanna sit for my Joey?"

"Sure. I'd love to." Her baby Joey had blue eyes, too; only his hair was black and curly, and his skin wasn't as dark. He smiled at me from his high chair. I walked up to play with him. He was adorable. He looked clean and smelled from talcum powder—not from urine like Beebe, Millie's baby sister. "When would you want me to sit for you, Mrs. Garcia?"

"On Friday afternoon for about two hours."

I figured Mama wouldn't mind. I'd be home before Shabbas. "Friday would be great. I could be here a quarter after three."

Mrs. Garcia asked, "Would ten cents an hour be okay?"

"Oh, yes, that will be fine. Thanks, Mrs. Garcia." I turned to leave. "I'll see you on Friday, then. Bye."

Francy and I walked out holding hands. "Thank you for recommending me, Francy."

"You're welcome. And Leely, whenever you're here, like on the weekends, you can always practice on our piano. Remember, you've already had your first lesson."

"Oh, I'll remember all right! Gosh! I lost track of time. I bet my father will be worried I've been gone so long. Ha-a-h!" My hand flew to my mouth. "And the girls, they probably got tired of waiting and went home." I straddled Papa's delivery bike. "I'll see you, Francy." I waved and rode off.

With the breeze blowing on my face, I smiled all the way back to the market. I had had my first piano lesson, and I wanted to shout it out to the world.

11 Best Friends

JOEY WAS AN ADORABLE BABY TO SIT FOR. He giggled and laughed and played ball with me. When we played hide and seek he called, "Leely, Leely, find me." But what he liked the most was sitting on my lap and turning the pages while I read a book.

Throughout the two hours I spent baby-sitting Francy ran in, played with us for a few minutes, then returned to stay with her father.

When Francy came in again she said, "My mother just got home, so I can stay now." She sat with us while I finished reading the story of "Henny Penny, The Sky Is Falling."

Shortly afterwards Mrs. Garcia returned. Our mouths dropped open. She had her hair bleached platinum blond, and she looked strangely different.

"Do you like it?" she asked going to the mirror. She fluffed the bottom of her hair and turned to us, smiling for approval.

"It's the same color and style as the movie actress, Jean Harlow," I commented. Francy and I nodded our heads. I looked at Francy's crooked smile and hoped I didn't look as shocked as she did. But I was sure I did.

"We'll have to get used to it—you look so different," Francy said. "You don't look like Mrs. Garcia anymore."

"You think so? I hope my husband likes it. He adores Jean Harlow."

Unable to remove my eyes from the mashed potatoes Mrs. Garcia kept fluffing on top of her head, I assured her that Joey had been no problem and thanked her for the twenty cents. "Do you want me to come again next week, Mrs. Garcia?" I asked hopefully.

"Definitely! I've already made my appointment at the beauty parlor for the same time next week."

"Great! So I'll see you then. Bye, Joey." I wheeled around to give him a hug and kiss.

We climbed over the porch divider that separated the Garcias' house and Francy's. "Francy, do you like Mrs. Garcia's hair?"

"No! I think it's awful. Do you?"

"Me, too. Her skin looks green under that hair."

We were laughing when we entered Francy's kitchen. Mrs. Piccolo was at the sink. She was a pretty woman of average height, pleasantly plump, with thick black hair she wore in a bun at the nape of her neck. She had the same creamy complexion as Francy.

"What are you girls laughing so hysterically about?"

"Mama, Mrs. Garcia bleached her hair platinum blond."

Mrs. Piccolo closed her eyes and crossed herself. "*Mamma mia,* with her dark skin?" She crossed herself again. "Does she look a mess?"

"Yesss!" We both burst out laughing again.

"It's a shame." Mrs. Piccolo shook her head. "Tsk, tsk, tsk—what women will do to please their husbands."

Francy said, "You should see her husband, Leely. He is so-o-o handsome."

"He must be rich, too, if he can afford for her to go to the beauty parlor each week and hire a babysitter."

"It's not his money, it's hers. That's why he married her. Right, Mama?"

"Francy, that's enough! It's not nice to gossip."

"Yeah," I said, "let's not be *yentas.*" I looked out the window. "Whoops! It's getting dark. I gotta run. See you tomorrow, Francy."

"I'll call for you in the morning." Francy closed the door behind me.

Francy arrived after breakfast carrying two brown paper bags. "For the leaves," she said, tucking one under her arm and one under mine.

"Good idea!" I grabbed my coat, and we left for the park.

The leaves were as bright and crisp as the fall day. The sun was shining, a dry breeze was blowing, and there was a chill in the air reminding us that winter was on its way. We enjoyed picking leaves so much, we didn't realize how fast the time went.

"We sure got a large assortment of leaves, didn't we, Leely?"

"Two bags full. Some of them are new to me. I never saw so many different colors and shapes. Probably because so few trees grow in Brooklyn."

We were walking home with our harvest of autumn leaves. "We don't go to the park often enough," Francy said. "It's as close to the country as we can get. We should go more. It's good to get away from the drab buildings and cement sidewalks."

"Yes, to the softness of green grass, shrubs, and flowers," I added. "Even the little lake in the park is a pleasant change from the oceans of gray streets." We looked at each other and chuckled. "Are we creating a poem?" I asked.

"Maybe we're painting a picture," Francy said, "but let's keep going. It's fun. In the park we can escape the smell of garbage cans and cooking odors."

"My turn." I looked around the street for clues. "And the stench of horse manure." We laughed. "And gasoline from honking cars."

We giggled and tittered and jabbed each other playfully. Francy continued, "Run away to the park where the clouds are not screened with smoke."

"Listen for the chirp of birds instead of sirens and clanging fire engines." We went on and on, swinging our brown paper bags filled with colorful leaves as we swaggered home.

"I'm going to let my father help me pick out the most unusual leaves for our table. He'll enjoy doing that. What about your parents, Leely. Do you think they will like it if you decorate your dinner table with leaves?"

I gave that some serious thought. "No, I really don't! They'll probably think it's dirt and say, 'Why is there *shmutz* on the table?' My mother hates dirt!" We laughed.

"My mother hates dirt, too, but she loves nature." Francy turned to look at me. "She's always bringing something home: a flower, an acorn, a tree pod, blossoms from a bush...different nature things."

I nodded thoughtfully. "Well, now that I think about it, my parents have told me stories of when they were children and lived near farms in Russia. They may have been poor, but the countryside was beautiful. Hills, forests, lakes—all the richness of nature." I sighed. "Too bad they were forced to leave. They ran for their lives when the Cossacks, Russian soldiers, rode their horses through the Jewish settlements, burning, beating, torturing—murdering any Jew in their way."

"Why did they do that?" Francy was all ears.

"In Russia there were pogroms—organized attacks against Jews. The leaders of the government encouraged it. They wanted the peasants to blame their troubles on the Jews."

"Whew! That's terrible! I'm glad that didn't happen in Italy. The Italians came here to earn more money and make a better life for themselves. They were poor, too, but they weren't murdered."

"And you know what I noticed, Francy? No matter how poor the Italians are, most Italians seem to have gardens. They grow vegetables, herbs, fig trees, flowers. They brought their love for nature with them, didn't they?"

"You bet! And their love for music, too." Francy thrust her chest out.

"Maybe I will place some leaves on the dinner table. My parents just might appreciate it."

We arrived at Maple Street, and Francy asked, "Did you put Mrs. Garcia's twenty cents in your *kenippel*, Leely?"

"I should say so! I won't leave my money around anymore. I'm not taking a chance of finding it gone again."

"How much money have you got so far?" Francy watched the growth of my savings with great interest.

"Forty-nine cents. Another eleven cents and I can buy the taillight."

"Can I go with you to buy it?"

"Sure. You can join Millie and Irene a-a-nd Adeline—they want to come, too."

Francy stopped walking. She looked directly into my face and asked, "Are you suspicious of Adeline, Leely?"

"Umm...I'm not saying anything. My mother said if you don't see it with your own eyes, you mustn't accuse anybody. And my sister Evy said anything I may be thinking of is only circumstantial evidence, because it can't be proven."

"They're right, Leely. You really don't know who took it."

From down the street, racing toward us on his bike, Philly waved and called our names. He stopped short at our feet, out of breath from pedaling fast. "Leely, where've you been? I've been riding all around the neighborhood looking for you."

"Francy and I have been in the park picking autumn leaves."

"I know. Your mother told me. I went to the park and couldn't find you. I'm riding around and around the streets looking for you."

"Well, here I am! What's up?"

"The older guys, Yussy and his friends, and your sister Evy and her friends are having a bonfire. They won't let us in on it, so we're gonna have our own. Do you two want in on it?"

I looked at Francy and shrugged my shoulders. "When?"

"Where?" Francy asked.

"Tonight. It has to be when it gets dark. And it's in the empty lot next to your house."

"A bonfire, huh? And you're sure my sister is gonna be there?"

Philly nodded. "I know. I heard them making plans." Philly closed his blue eyes and pointed his nose to the sky. "They said we're too young to socialize with them."

"Well, if Evy is going, then my mother should let me go. What about you, Francy?"

"Well," she said, shrugging her shoulders, "if you're going, then I guess my mother will let me go, too."

"Okay, good!" Philly said happily. "Now you have to bring something for the bonfire: a potato to cook a mickey, marshmallows to roast, or anything you've got that you can share with everybody."

Francy's face fell. "I can't bring marshmallows, Philly. I don't have the money to buy them."

I said, "I can bring two potatoes. We've got them in the house. What about the other girls. Are they invited?"

"Oh yeah, I already saw Millie and Irene and told them about it. But I still have to tell some of my friends." Philly got ready to leave.

"Is Frankie gonna be there?" Francy asked.

"Sure! He's one of us guys."

"How about my kid brother, Carmine? Can I bring him?"

"No! He's too young! I gotta go now. We have a lot of preparing to do." Quickly Philly rode away.

Francy and I chuckled "Hmm. He's no different from his brother, is he?" Francy said.

"Of course not! He imitates everything Yussy says and does."

"Let's go to my house first, Leely. I want to make sure my mother will allow me to go to the bonfire."

Francy's mother was preparing lunch. "How was the park, girls? Nice?"

"Oh, yes, beautiful. Just like up in the mountains." I closed my eyes and visualized the mountains in the fall covered with warm autumn colors.

"Mama, the kids on the block are making a bonfire in the lot next to Leely's house. They invited me to go."

"I don't like fires, Francy. They're dangerous."

"The older brothers and sisters are going to be there, too, Mama."

I spoke up. "And knowing my mother, she'll poke her head in every now and then."

Mrs. Piccolo cocked her head to the side and studied the two of us. "Well, if your sister is going to be there, and if your mother checks, it should be all right. What are they going to roast?"

"We have to bring a potato or marshmallow or anything to share. What can I bring, Mama?"

Mrs. Piccolo flipped her head to the other side and thought for a moment. "How about something to drink, like lemonade or iced tea?"

"Wow! That would be great! I bet nobody will think of something to drink. Let's not tell them, Francy. You just surprise them."

Carmine piped up, "Can I go, too, Mama?"

"No, this is for big children, Carmine. You don't belong with Francy and her friends on weekends." Grateful, Francy hugged her mother.

Mr. Piccolo called Francy from his bedroom. She went in to see what her father wanted and came back smiling. "My father wants to hear you play the scales."

I hurried into the living room to please him. I put my finger on middle C and went up and down the treble scale saying each note out loud, with Francy telling me when to turn my thumb under. I did it a number of times, and my fingers moved faster. Soon I was turning my thumb on my own.

Mr. Piccolo called out, "That's good, Leely. Now you gotta learn with the left hand." Then he had a coughing spell. I went to the bedroom door and threw him a kiss.

Mrs. Piccolo said, "Girls, have some lunch."

"Will you have lunch with me, Leely?"

"I don't know. I didn't tell my mother I wouldn't be home for lunch…but I didn't tell her I would, either."

"Come, have a bowl of minestrone soup." Mrs. Piccolo placed two bowls on the table.

Carmine was already eating his. "Eat with us, Leely."

Having never eaten minestrone soup, I didn't know what to expect. I picked up a spoonful and tasted it. "Hey, it's vegetable soup! And it's delicious. Just like my mother's, except for the macaroni."

Mrs. Piccolo smiled. "You know the Italians—they're the only people who cook everything with pasta." She sat down to eat with us.

I thought about that for a while, then said, "No, they're not! Lookit!" I counted on my fingers. "My mother makes noodles for chicken soup and noodle *kugel*. She makes *kreplach,* and she uses the same elbow macaroni as you have here in your soup. We eat them with pot cheese."

Mrs. Piccolo looked at me, tilting her head to the side, something she seemed to do often. "That's very interesting. I never knew that."

"What's *kreplach?*" Francy asked.

"They're little dumplings made of dough and stuffed with meat or potatoes or cheese. We put them in our soup or eat them cooked with onions sauteed in butter."

The three Piccolo heads shot up from their soup, and together they sang out, "Ravioli!"

Joey jumped up and ran to the refrigerator. He brought out a bowl and lifted the cover for me to see. "Like these?"

"Yup! But ours are round and joined on top."

"Gnocchi!" They nodded their heads. For a few moments nobody spoke. We just looked at each other and smiled. It felt good.

"Mrs. Piccolo, can Francy have supper with me tonight? It's Saturday night—that's deli night. We usually have it at our store. So does Adeline's family and the grocer's family. Even Frank Alonzo the fish man's family comes in. They eat kosher deli, too. The market is all lit up. It's a lot of fun."

"What's the delicatessen you eat?" Mrs. Piccolo asked as she removed the empty soup bowls.

"Oh, all kinds: corned beef, pastrami, salami, tongue. We have sour pickles and mustard and cream or celery soda."

"Oh, can I please eat with Leely, Mama, please?"

Mrs. Piccolo had the kindest smile. "Okay, go! It'll do you good to get out of the house. You're a good girl, Francy. You deserve a treat. But don't walk home alone in the dark. Make sure somebody takes you home."

"Philly Bronson can take her home."

"Or Frankie Leone—he lives a couple of houses away. He's a good friend of Philly's," Francy said, squirming a little in her seat.

On our way to my house, we met Frankie coming out of his. "Hi Francy, Leely. You girls gonna be at the bonfire tonight?"

"Yeah, are you?" Francy blushed.

Frankie had straight black hair and brown eyes. He was cute. He also bounced on his toes when he walked, just like Philly did. "Yeah, I'm bringing marshmallows. What're you bringing?"

Francy zipped her mouth closed. "I can't tell you. It's a secret." Quickly her face lit up—she thought of something. She whispered in my ear, "His father sells ices and ice cream in paper cups. We could ask him to bring cups for the lemonade."

"Good idea! Ask him."

"Frankie, I'm going to tell you what I'm bringing because we'd like you to bring something we need for it, but you must promise to keep it a secret."

"Okay, I'm good with secrets."

"I'm bringing lemonade."

"Terrific! We're sure to get thirsty from all the mickies and marshmallows."

"Only we have no cups." Francy looked at Frankie hopefully.

Frankie waved the thought away. "No problem. I'll bring the cups." Frankie looked down at his shoes, then up again at Francy. "Hey, Francy, do you want me to help you carry the lemonade?"

I watched Francy's face turn red again. "Okay, thanks! I'm gonna have dinner with Leely at her father's store."

"And I'm gonna be helping Philly and the boys set up the bonfire. I'll come by and pick you up when we're finished."

I finally said something. "Frankie, don't forget it's a secret."

"I won't. I've got to help find wood for the fire. See you later." Frankie waved goodbye and took off on his bike.

"Francy Piccolo, why didn't you tell me you liked Frankie?"

Francy opened her mouth to speak, but nothing came out. After a few moments she said, "Well, it was my secret, and I didn't think I should tell anybody."

"But I'm your best friend. And I told you about Philly."

"Okay, so now we know each other's secrets." Francy took my hand and we swung our arms as we walked.

12 The Bonfire

SATURDAY EVENING AT DUSK THE SABBATH WAS OVER AND WE were all on our way with Francy to the butcher store. The empty lot next to our building was filled with activity. Boys were busy pulling and pushing wooden crates filled with sticks, newspapers, and branches. Other kids were whittling points on long twigs. There was no question that something important was going on.

Papa stopped to watch. "What's happening here?"

I expanded my chest and smiled. "They're making a bonfire."

"A fire? What do you need with a bonfire?" he asked.

"We'll make mickies—they're roasted potatoes," Evy answered.

"And toasted marshmallows. Yummy!" Arnie licked his lips and rubbed his belly.

"We'll sing songs, " I said.

"And have fun," Francy added.

Mama frowned. "I don't like fires; they're dangerous."

"Don't be apprehensive, Mother," Evy tried to reassure Mama with her highfalutin' vocabulary (her boyfriends were nearby). "We're not babies, you know."

"Apprensive, shmensive, accidents could happen, no? A child could slip, get pushed, just playing, her clothes could catch on fire, no? With children, anything could happen. I don't like it, Jacob."

"Well, nothing is going to happen but fun. We'll be extra special careful," I said, hoping to convince Mama.

For a moment, Papa forgot he had to get to work. He stood chuckling and watching all that was going on.

When Evy walked over to Donald and the boys to give them her potato, Philly and Frankie ran up to us. They spoke softly, covering the sides of their mouths with their hands. Philly looked around to make sure his brother Yussy and his buddies couldn't hear. "Wait till you see the nice boxes we have to sit on. We took all the crates in the market except for the smelly fish boxes."

Frankie said, "And we asked Adeline to tell her father not to give any crates to the big shots over there." He pointed his thumb to the older boys. "Her father saved them all for us."

Still whispering at the side of his hand, Philly added, "This is gonna be swell. We'll all be sitting, and the big shots will have to stand. Don't tell your sister."

I gave Philly two potatoes, which he took back to the lot. Then Frankie whispered to Francy, "I'll call for you at the butcher store, and we'll go for the lemonade and cups."

Papa seemed tickled with what he saw and heard. He shook his head and said, "Only in America. Only in America can children be free to play with all kinds of children in the neighborhood—and get along so nicely together. Right, Riva?"

"Only in America!" Mama repeated. "Still, I think fires are dangerous."

"*Nu*, let's go, *kinder*, it's getting late." Papa walked away, still smiling."Only in America."

"Mother, if you don't mind, could we please eat right away so we could be back as soon as it gets dark?"

"We can't eat right away, Evy. I have to help Papa cut meat for the counter and windows. After I do that we'll go to the delicatessen store for sandwiches."

"Then we'll help so you can get finished sooner. Okay, kids?"

"Absolutely," I answered.

"Absolutely," Arnie mimicked.

"Absolutely," Francy agreed. "This is going to be fun, Leely, being a part of your family."

Mama and Papa put clean white aprons on top of their starched white jackets. Each worked on a wooden butcher block. They cut chops, steaks, and slices of liver. As they cut, Evy and I placed the meat on trays and handed the trays to Francy, who put them in the showcase and windows.

Papa gave instructions where and how to place the meat and trays, and we followed them. We worked in an assembly line, passing trays from one to another and calling out like surgeons in an operating room: "Lamb chops! Paper! Tray!" Each of us tried to be faster

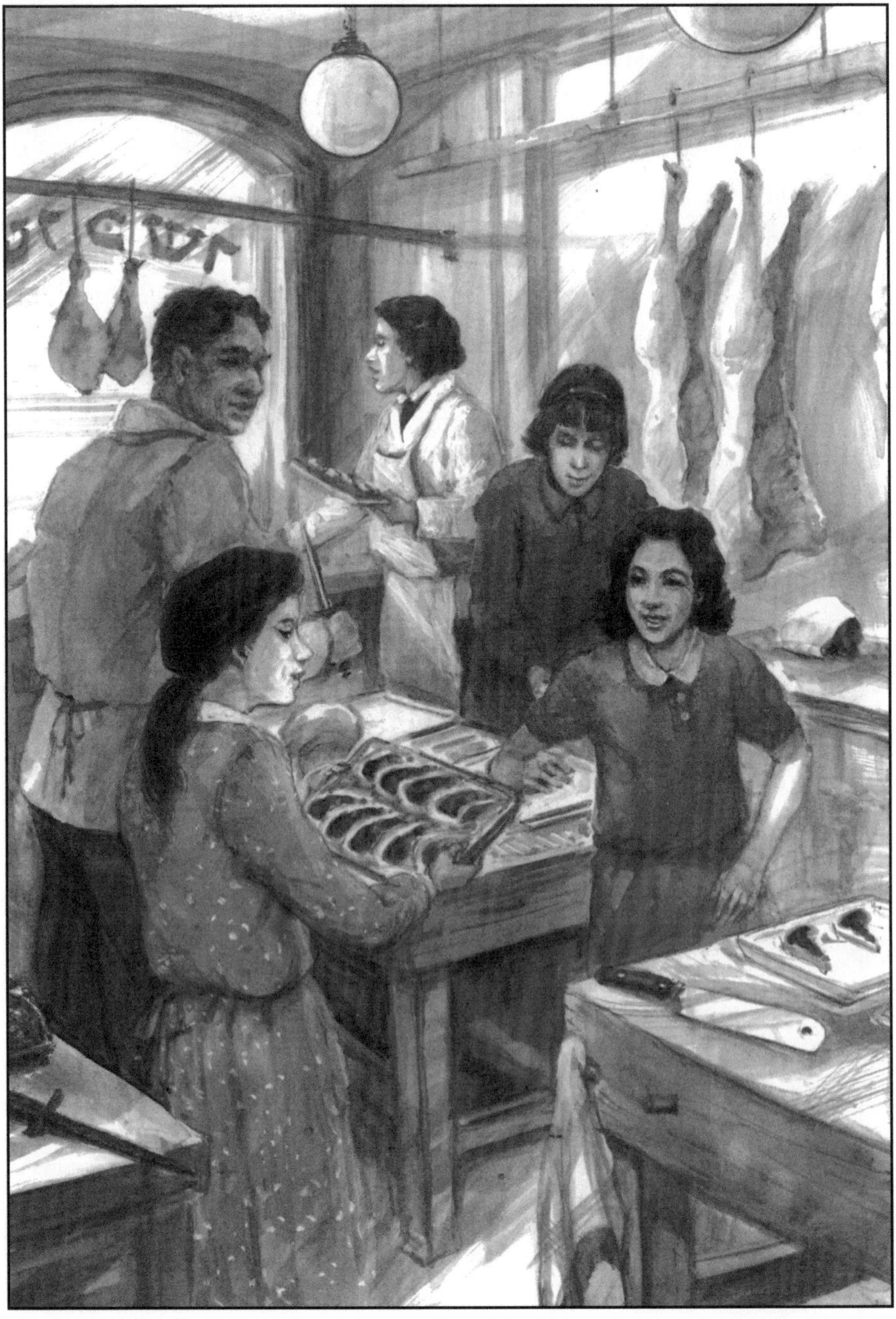

than the other. We giggled, we teased, Mama and Papa laughed, and before we knew it, the store was ready for business.

Mama brought back different meats from the delicatessen store. We helped her carry the bottles of celery and cream soda. All of us stood around the white enamel table waiting for her to slice the Jewish rye bread for sandwiches. We moaned with each whiff of the mouth-watering smoked meats. Francy got a taste of each meat so she could choose which she liked the best.

"Mm, they're all so good," she said, licking her lips. "I think I like the hot pastrami best."

"Smart girl," Papa said. "I like it best, too."

The mustard came in small cone-shaped waxed papers. We showed Francy how to squeeze upward from the narrow point at the bottom. As usual, it squirted all over our fingers. And as usual, we complained about the mess, licking our fingers, hungrily biting into the delicious sandwiches.

Adeline came up front from her father's section of the store. She, too, was eating a deli sandwich. "What kind do you have, Francy?"

"Hot pastrami. What kind do you have?"

"Chicken salami." Adeline gave us a taste of her chicken salami in return for a bite out of our corned beef and tongue sandwiches and a slice of sour pickle.

When we finished eating we waited for Evy to leave, then Adeline and I picked up the crates her father had saved for us. They were big and clumsy. We put one into another, and between the two of us we managed to carry them to the bonfire. Francy and Frankie went for the lemonade.

Four bonfires were glowing in the night. We had two, just like the older kids. Our friends were already sitting on the boxes the boys had brought the wood and papers in earlier. We put the crates we carried around both fires.

"Sit down fast!" Philly said, pushing me down on a crate, "before the big shots come and take them." I glanced over to the other kids. They had their hands on their hips as they gaped at us.

"Hey," Donald called out, "where did you get those boxes?"

"Yeah, Philly," Yussy hollered, "just where did you get them? The fruit man said he didn't have any extra crates."

"Oh, we have connections," Philly answered, crossing his arms on his chest. The rest of us tittered behind our hands.

The big shots ogled us even more as we cheered Francy and Frankie when they arrived with the surprise lemonade. Everybody's smiling face reflected the orange glow of the fire. We passed the marshmallows around, stuck them on pointed twigs, and held them over the fires. When they were toasted black we ate them off the sticks, but they stuck like glue to our lips and hands. They were a delicious gooey mess.

"Did anybody think of bringing napkins?" Millie asked.

"Aw, wipe it on your clothes. The napkin would only stick to your fingers anyway," Red said.

"Yeah, the only thing that will take the sticky marshmallow off your fingers is your tongue," Moish said. With that, all of us began licking our fingers.

We laughed and kidded around. Red said, "I'm surprised Tony's gang of bullies hasn't tried to break up the bonfire yet."

"Well, they'll be here soon for sure. They only live down the end of the block, and Schnoz has a nose for smelling out places where people are having fun," Millie said.

Irene said, "They're always starting fights. I hope they don't bother us tonight."

"Look, don't worry," Philly said, "they're probably having their own bonfire in the lot on Kinsgton Avenue. But if they do start up, relax. We have enough guys here who can handle them. If they look for trouble, we'll give it to them."

Adeline suggested, "Let's start singing 'Home on the Range.'" We began to sing completely off-key. We sounded like screeching cats. It was so bad, we had to cover our ears. Fortunately Francy, coming from a musical family, sang beautifully. She raised her voice loud enough to lead us. Smiling with pride, we finished singing "Home on the Range" in the proper key. We were so busy having fun, we forgot about the big shots at the other bonfire. Until Evy came over.

"Leely, how about sharing a seat with one of your friends and giving me one crate? My friend Trudy and I are tired of standing, and we don't want to sit on the dirt with the fellows. What do you say, huh?"

I looked at Philly, shrugged my shoulders, and slipped onto the crate next to me. I shared it with Irene.

"Thanks!" Evy gave me a peck on the cheek.

"What's the matter, big shots?" Philly called over to them. "You didn't think we were good enough to join you, so now that we did better than you, you send the girls to do your dirty work. You too embarrassed to do it yourself?" Nobody answered Philly, but we heard a murmur as their heads bent toward the ground. Our faces, glowing in the light of the fire, smirked with satisfaction.

Just then Mama appeared, holding Arnie's hand. She was still wearing her long white apron. She walked from Evy's bonfire to ours. Satisfied that all was going well at both fires, she smiled and patted me on the shoulder. Arnie's cheeks were oozing with white sugar from the toasted marshmallows. He poked me on the arm and pointed to his mouth. I gave him another marshmallow, toasted black on the outside. He gave me a sticky kiss in return.

"Hey, guys! My mickey should be ready; it was the first one in." Moish probed with his stick for the first potato in the row.

"It figures you'd get hungry first, Moish," Red said. "You're always eating." Moish looked it, too. He was exceptionally chubby.

"This one is mine." Moish pulled out a black mickey. He brought it to his mouth and bit through the thick burnt jacket.

"Yikes! It's hot!" Moish screamed, throwing the hot potato into the air. It fell back into the fire. Moish danced around like a clown avoiding fire crackers. His tongue hung out, and his hands fanned it rapidly.

"Francy, quick—the lemonade!" I called. Francy poured some lemonade into a paper cup and gave it to Moish. He took a long gulp, then stuck his tongue into it to soak. He looked so comical, we cracked up.

Evy and Yussy came over to see what had happened. Evy said, "Let me see. Does it burn badly?"

Moish took his tongue out of the lemonade. "Yeth, it burnth real bad."

Evy looked. "The tip of your tongue is very red. I wouldn't soak it in lemonade if I were you."

"The acid in the lemon will only make it burn more," Yussy said, trying not to laugh at Moish's expressions.

Philly walked up to Moish and put his hand on Moish's shoulder. "You're named after Moses, aren't you, Moish?" Moish nodded. "Well, you know, Moish, there's this story that Moses burned his tongue when he was a child." Philly looked around for recognition, and we all nodded our heads. "It left him with a lisp for the rest of his life."

"With a speech impediment," Evy corrected.

I said, "And his brother, Aaron, had to do all his talking for him. Especially when he spoke to the Pharaoh."

With his arm around Moish, Philly continued his story. "So figure like this: If you should remain with a speech impediment, you could very well be the Messiah the Jews have been waiting for for thousands of years. Another Moses!" We were all convulsed with laughter. Moish playfully shoved Philly away, his tongue still hanging out of his mouth.

Laughing, Evy and Yussy returned to their bonfires as we began digging into our fires for our mickies. Francy's and mine were ready. We broke them open with our marshmallow twigs and let them cool. The insides were white and fluffy like whipped cream.

"This is the most delicious potato I ever ate in my whole life!" I exclaimed. "It doesn't need butter or salt."

"Mine, too!" Francy agreed. We even thought the thick burnt jackets tasted great.

Soon the older kids were singing "Row, Row, Row Your Boat." We picked up the next line, "gently down the stream," and together we all sang, "merrily, merrily, merrily, merrily, life is but a dream." Joyously, we sang faster and louder as we repeated the song.

We saw a short, fat, bald-headed man standing between the two sets of bonfires. His arms waved, and his mouth moved quickly. We stopped singing. That's when we heard his shouting.

"What do you think you're doing here?" the man's voice bellowed across the entire lot.

"Having a bonfire," everybody shouted back.

"Yeah? Well, you can't have it anymore. Put the fires out and get out of here."

"What?" we cried out.

"Who are you?" Yussy asked.

"I'm the landlord, that's who."

"Landlord of what? There's no house here," Evy said.

"I own this land. The property is mine, and I want you all off it—*now*!" The man had a coarse, loud voice that echoed from the sides of the buildings. It was threatening and scary. The kids remained silent.

Then Donald spoke up. "Mister, we don't know who you are or what you are. We're not harming anything or anybody, and we have no intention of leaving the premises."

"That's telling him!" Philly shouted.

"Yeah!" everybody cheered.

"If you don't put the fires out and leave, I'm calling the police."

"Go ahead!" Yussy said. "See if we care!"

"Okay, I will!" The mean old man turned to leave and came face to face with Officer O'Leary, our neighborhood cop, who appeared like magic out of the darkness. It became so quiet you could hear the fires crackle.

Officer O'Leary was big, Irish, and friendly. "What's the problem here?" he asked.

"Boy! I'm lucky you're here. I was just going to call the police."

"So I heard you say. Tell me, my good man, what's your complaint?"

"These kids are disrupting the peace."

"You don't say? Now, just how're they doing that?"

"They're noisy and rowdy."

"Noisy and rowdy, you say? Well, I'll be telling you, I've been standing across the street watching these young ones, and I ain't seen them do one rowdy or improper thing. The only noise they've been making is singing. And that, sir, is about the healthiest noise one could want to hear from kids."

We kids were all smiles. The cop was on our side.

"I own this property, and I want them off."

"Well now, how do I know that you own this property?"

"I can prove it I've got the papers."

"Have you, now? Do you wanna go fetch them and show them to me?"

The man hesitated. "I can't. They're locked in the bank."

"Well, now, that's too bad, ain't it? But I'll be telling you what," Officer O'Leary said, putting his arm on the man's shoulder. "If you're the landlord, these kids are doing you a favor, they are. Look at it this way, mister—they're burning the weeds for you and probably doing away with a lot of rats."

"No way! They're leaving a dirty mess from the fire and food."

"Okay. You kids have to clean up all the dirt when you get finished. Remove all the trash so there's no sign of a bonfire ever having been here. If it ain't all removed tonight, be back tomorrow and finish the job. Is that understood?"

"Yes, Officer O'Leary!" Everybody understood.

The policeman, with his arm still around the landlord's shoulder, walked him away, talking softly to him. The man pointed to the windows on the second floor that were on the side of the building facing the lot. Everybody looked up to see what he was pointing to.

"That's probably where he lives," Donald said.

"I hope he sells this lot and somebody builds a house on it—smack up against his building," Yussy shouted.

"Right! And blocks the sun and fresh air from his windows," I said.

"That's right!" We all laughed.

Officer O'Leary returned alone, wearing a broad smile. All his teeth were showing.

"Three cheers for Officer O'Leary!" Yussy shouted.

"Hip, hip, hurray! Hip, hip, hurray! Hip, hip, hurray!"

Evy and her girlfriends started to sing "For He's a Jolly Good Fellow," and we joined in:

> For he's a jolly good fellow,
> For he's a jolly good fellow,
> For he's a jolly good fell-o-o-o-w,
> That, nobody can deny.

"Hey, Officer, O'Leary, you wanna mickey?"

"Well, now, my boy, I thought you'd never ask."

The big shots gave him a mickey, and we brought him a cup of lemonade. Everyone gathered around him, patted him, and cheered him again.

"Don't any of you make a liar out of me, now. I want to see this lot nice and clean come tomorrow morning. Hear now?"

"Yeah, we hear!"

Frankie said, "We'll be happy to clean up. In fact, we'll whistle while we work. Right, guys?"

"Right!" Then he began to sing the song from *Snow White and the Seven Dwarfs*.

> We'll whistle while we work.
> Tra la la la la la la!

Frankie threw his arms up and kicked. Everybody joined him, and in no time we had a snake line dancing around the four bonfires, all of us singing as we danced.

13 Bad News

SUNDAY MORNING AFTER THE BONFIRE THE LOT WAS FULL OF KIDS again. We kept our promise to Officer O'Leary to clean it up. Everybody showed. That is, everybody except Francy.

"Hey, Leely, where's Francy?" Millie asked.

"Gee, I don't know. Maybe she went to church," I said as I dropped a piece of charred wood into the trash box. Philly followed with a shovel full of ashes.

Officer O'Leary arrived. He stood with his legs apart and his arms folded, nodding his head in approval. "A better bunch of kids I've never seen on my beat. I'm proud of you. You're an asset to the community! Go back and tell your parents I said so."

"Yeah!" we yelled as we dragged the rubbish to the curb. Then we turned to admire our work. "This is the cleanest lot in the borough of Brooklyn!"

"Three cheers for the pride of the neighborhood!" Donald

shouted. "Hip, hip, hurray! Hip, hip, hurray!" Everybody cheered happily.

"Okay, kids, go on home and have a good lunch," Officer O'Leary ordered as he patted the kids on their heads and backs.

"Yeah! Come on Yussy, let's go home and have a big lunch. I'm starved," Philly said, bouncing away on the soles of his sneakers. "See you guys later."

I could smell the aroma of Mama's leftover pot roast as we walked up the stairs. She had lunch ready. While we were eating we told her what the policeman had said. "*Nu,* maybe now the landlord won't be such a complainer. He has the cleanest lot in the neighborhood, no?"

"In New York," I added.

"Or on the planet," Evy said. "That landlord is ridiculous. Lots aren't supposed to be clean. It just isn't normal."

"I know," Arnie said. "It's an a-nom-aly, right, Evy?" We stared at Arnie, then laughed admiringly.

"Holy cow, Arnie! You remembered that word from such a long time ago," Evy said. "I'm so proud of you!" She got up and gave Arnie a kiss on his forehead.

"Sure I remember, because the cat I used to have, Rusty, had six toes, and you said it was an a-nom-aly. Remember?" Evy and I smiled and nodded our heads. Arnie showed his pride with a toothless grin.

I said, "Arnie, I'd give you a kiss on your nose, but the snot's running down to your mouth." Arnie's nose was always running.

While Arnie bit into a piece of *mondelbrot* Mama took a napkin to his nose. "Let me wipe," she said, "or you won't know if you're eating or drinking your *mondelbrot*." Mama made delicious *mondelbrot*. It was a crisp cake made with almonds that she sliced. We ate it like a cookie.

I was dunking my cake in applesauce when I heard footsteps run quickly up the stairs and stop at our door. We all looked up and waited for the knock. Someone pounded.

Mama knitted her brow. She called out, "Come in!"

The door opened in the foyer, and Philly stuck his face into the kitchen doorway. He was out of breath. "Leely! You know why Francy didn't come to help clean up the lot?" I shook my head. "Her father died during the night!"

"*Oh my God!*" I screamed, then I covered my mouth with my hand.

"*Vey is mir!*" Mama shouted, clutching her hands to her chest. "Such a terrible thing!"

"There's a gang of people in her house. Neighbors and relatives. Everyone is crying and everything."

I jumped out of my seat. "Mama, I want to be with Francy. Should I go?"

"Of course go! She'll want a friend with her."

I burst out crying. "And her father gave me my first piano lesson."

"Come on," Philly said. "I'll ride you over on my bike."

Still upset, I stuck the *mondelbrot* I'd been eating in Philly's hand and went to get my coat. Philly looked at the bitten cake and stuffed it in his mouth. His cheeks bulged as he chewed fast and furiously. Then his transparent blue eyes opened wide as he rolled his tongue across his lips.

Seeing how he liked it, Mama took another piece of *mondelbrot* from the cake plate and handed it to Philly.

"Mm, mm, it's good. Thanks!"

I sobbed through the ride to Francy's house. Philly talked and ate the cake.

There were a lot of people standing on the Piccolo porch. Inside, more were moving around; some were sitting, some standing; most were crying. We didn't see Francy. Philly and I looked in the kitchen. Women were fussing at the range amidst the delicious aroma of Italian cooking. Francy wasn't in the dining room either. We finally found her in the living room. She and Carmine sat on the couch, their mother in between them. Their eyes were red from crying.

I went up to them, biting my lip. Francy cried out, "Oh, Leely, I'm so glad you came!" I didn't know what to say, so I said nothing. The tears ran down my face.

I sat beside Francy and put my arm around her. "Of course I came. As soon as Philly told me. Hey, I'm your best friend, aren't I?" Francy nodded at me and then at Philly, tears gushing down her face.

Philly stood in front of us with his hands in his pockets, bouncing up and down on his heels. He looked as if he didn't know what to say, either. He watched the two of us cry.

"It's good of you to come, Leely," Mrs. Piccolo said, sniffing and wiping her tears at the same time. "It's good for Francy." I wiped my tears with the back of my hand. Francy held out a large man's handkerchief. It was wet, but I used it anyway.

Philly started to fidget. He looked around. Francy answered his unasked question. "He's being made ready for the coffin, and then they'll put his body on view. They're going to put the coffin over there." She pointed to a wall between two windows where a space was already cleared.

"So when's the funeral?" I asked.

"We don't know yet. Sometime this week."

Philly stopped bouncing on his heels. "You mean his body is gonna be here in the house for days?"

"Uh-huh." Francy started weeping again. Philly looked at me and rolled his eyes.

I placed both arms around Francy and rocked with her. I noticed her mother was rocking, too. People came over to talk to her, but I don't think she heard what they were saying. Her eyes were looking into space and she kept right on rocking and crying.

A beautiful old white-haired lady was sitting in an armchair sobbing quietly. She held a rosary in her hands. Every now and then she pounded her chest with her fist.

"Is that woman with the white hair your grandmother?" I asked.

"Yes, my father's mother."

"I thought so. There's a resemblance."

More people were coming in. Some of them were dropping envelopes into a basket on an end table.

"Francy," I whispered, "what are they putting into the basket?"

"Money for the funeral. We can't afford a funeral," Francy sobbed. I looked up at Philly. He was fidgeting with his hands again. I squirmed in my seat.

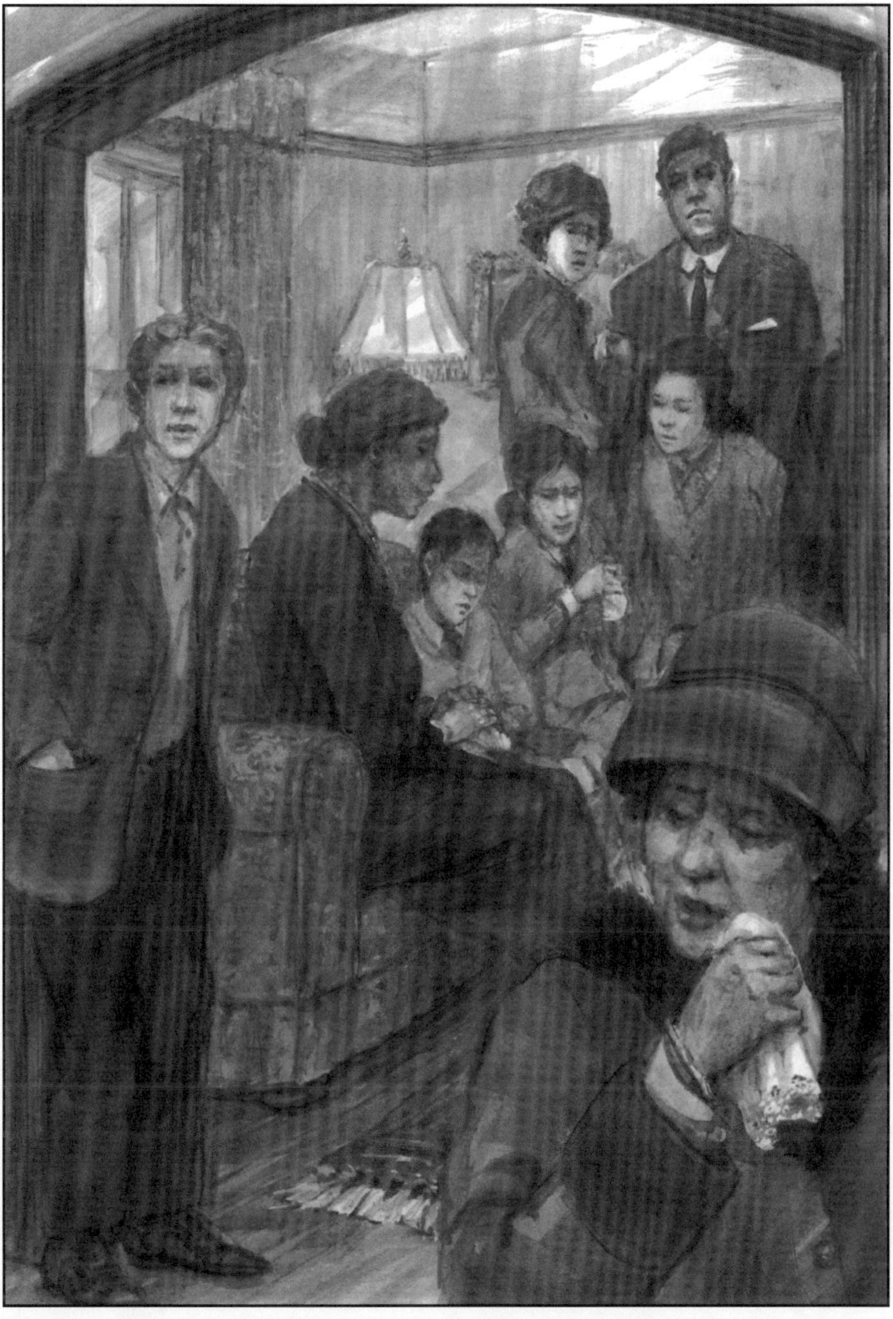

A man pulled a chair up to Mrs. Piccolo and sat in front of her. He spoke softly in her ear.

"My Uncle Al," Francy confided in me. I didn't hear what her uncle was saying, but Mrs. Piccolo whispered loud enough. "No, no insurance. Who could afford insurance?" She shook her head. "I haven't got a penny to my name. I'm not only a widow, I'm a poor widow. With two little children." She was crying and rocking again.

I looked at Francy's grandmother and noticed her facial expression change: Her skin tightened, her eyes closed, and her lips became hard lines. Then she let out a heart-rending cry in Italian, *"Dio Mio!"* She stood up from her chair, flung her arms up, and shook her fists at the ceiling. People came running from the other rooms. A long, loud wail sounded throughout the house as they tried to calm Francy's grandmother. She kept on wailing. Everybody cried.

I stood up. "Francy, I think we should leave. I feel in the way."

"No, please stay with me. I need you now."

I looked at Philly with confusion, not knowing what to do. He whispered in my ear, "I—I—I'll be outside in front of the house when you come out." His eyes were wet.

Francy ran over to her grandmother and threw her arms around her. Everyone stepped back. She sat her grandmother back into the chair and wiped her wrinkled face with a handkerchief. Slowly her grandmother calmed down.

I sat next to Carmine and took his hand. He looked up at me, pouting. "Why didn't Arnie come?"

"Today isn't a good time, Carmine. Maybe tomorrow."

Francy returned to her seat and held her mother's hand. People walked in and out of the room. They talked to Mrs. Piccolo, hugged and kissed Francy and Carmine, and dropped envelopes into the basket.

A woman and man came in carrying a small suitcase, which they dropped in the doorway. The woman ran to Francy's mother, letting out a wail. Mrs. Piccolo stood up. They hugged silently.

"Aunt Angie, my mother's sister. She lives in New Jersey. They're very close."

"They came with a suitcase. I suppose they're going to stay," I said.

"Yeah, and my grandmother and my father's brother, Joe, from Staten Island. And there's more coming from Manhattan, Little Italy. Do you know where that is?" Francy stuttered as she spoke.

"No, I don't. Where are they all going to sleep?" I asked.

"I guess all over the house. Some will go to my Aunt Rosa's house. She doesn't live too far. Carmine and I will probably sleep on the floor."

I sat there thinking. I knew they had three bedrooms, but no way did they have enough beds. "Francy, would you like to sleep in my house so there'll be more room?"

"I don't want to leave my mother. Thanks anyway!"

"I understand, Francy."

I could hear activity at the front door. The talking in the house subsided. One of the women from the kitchen walked up to Mrs. Piccolo and announced quietly, "The casket is here." Mrs. Piccolo tightened her lips and stiffened.

"Francy, are they gonna open the casket?" I meant to whisper, but I think I screamed.

"Sure. People have to say their last goodbye."

"Gosh!" To myself I thought, They're going to sit in the same room with the dead body! For days! Boy, I can imagine what will happen when they open the casket: The grandmother will scream again, everyone will cry and wail again, someone is bound to faint. I better get out of here before they bring the casket in.

"I'm gonna leave now, Francy, so your Aunt Angie can sit in my place. I'll see you after school tomorrow." I stood up and smiled at Aunt Angie, who was grateful for the seat. "Mrs. Piccolo, if it gets too crowded, Francy can come and stay in my house. My parents would be glad to have her."

"Thank you, Leely. I appreciate it, but I want Francy with me right now."

I nodded, blew Francy a kiss, and turned to leave. Too late! The casket was being carried through the long, narrow hall. I pressed back against the living room wall and sucked in my breath to let them pass. I peeked from the side of my eye. Oh, thank God! I thought. The lid is closed. I turned and ran down the hall out to the street.

Philly was waiting for me. "Did you see Mr. Piccolo?"

"No. I got out just in time."

A chilling scream sounded from the house. Philly and I nodded our heads, and together we said, "Mr. Piccolo."

I blew a deep breath. "Whew! I'm going home."

"Wanna ride?"

"No, thanks! I'll walk. I feel sort of sad inside, and my head hurts from crying. Maybe the walk will help."

"Okay, I'll walk you home." Philly bounced in his sneakers as he walked alongside me. We talked about death. He told me about his grandmother, who had died seven years before. "She died too late in the afternoon to be buried the same day. They placed her body in the front parlor, on the floor with lighted candles at her feet and head, and a man sat all night in the same room, praying. I was so scared I stayed in the back bedroom and I wouldn't come out until they buried her the next morning."

By the time I got home I felt worse. There the conversation about death continued for the rest of the day and into the evening. This was the first time we three kids had ever experienced a death, and we asked a lot of questions. Never having seen a dead person, I shuddered at the horror of spending three days and nights in the same house with a dead body.

Papa and Mama eased my anxiety by explaining that Jewish people bury their dead as soon as possible. Papa told me about some of the Jewish mourning traditions, such as covering all the mirrors in the house and sitting *shiva* for seven days.

"But the tragedy and the pain of losing a father or any other member of the family is the same, no matter what religion," Papa said.

Mama cried as she spoke. "The poor children! So young to be orphans. And all day they'll be alone while Mrs. Piccolo is working. We'll let the children stay with us as much as possible." Mama put her hand to her cheek. "*Oy vey,* tsk, tsk, tsk."

There was a knock at the door. Papa answered it. "Hello, Francy!"

She was standing with her Uncle Al. "Leely, it really got overcrowded in my house. There aren't enough blankets and stuff. My Uncle Al walked me over because it's dark out."

"Come in! Come in!" Mama called out. Francy's uncle introduced himself. "Will it be too much trouble if Francy sleeps here for the night? It really got heavy with relatives, and Francy preferred to stay here rather than anywhere else. She gave her bed to Grandma."

"No, no, she's welcome. Please not to worry," Mama said.

"How is Mrs. Piccolo?" Papa asked. "She's all right? Such a fine lady. Tsk, tsk, tsk."

"How could she be all right? She lost such a young, wonderful, talented husband. A terrible tragedy. Terrible! Terrible!" He handed Francy the paper bag he carried. "Here are your clothes, sweetheart. Try to get a good night sleep. Thank you for having her."

"We're happy we could help. Tell her mama she'll be okay here. And please tell Mrs. Piccolo we send our…our, uh…"

"Condolences," Evy called out.

"Yes, condolences," Mama finished. Uncle Al left, and we all fussed over Francy. Mama said, "Evy, you sleep with Arnie so Leely and Francy can sleep together. Jacob, maybe we could get the folding bed from your sister Sarah?"

"I didn't know Sarah had a folding bed. You like hot chocolate milk, Francy?" Papa asked. Francy nodded and smiled. "Riva, make hot chocolate for the children."

"I'll make for everybody and we can drink it with *mondelbrot* or *moon* cookies."

Nobody spoke about the death; we wanted to make it easier for Francy. But when we got into bed Francy talked and cried a lot. We compared the differences between Catholic and Jewish religious practices.

"When someone dies in the Jewish religion, after the funeral the mourners sit *shiva*. That's a Hebrew word for seven. Mourners sit for seven days."

"What do you mean you sit *shiva*?"

"That's how we mourn. My father told me the immediate family sits on low wooden stools, close to the earth, to be as near as we can to the one who was buried."

Francy said, "We mourn for the three days the body is laid out before the funeral." Francy started to whimper. I put my arm around her and kept talking.

"We cover all the mirrors in the house so we can't see our image."

"Why do you do that?"

"We're not supposed to be vain or aware of our appearance when mourning. And you know what else?"

"Mm?"

"They used to make a tear in their clothes before the funeral, but now they cut a black ribbon. My father said it comes from the Bible. Job tore his clothes when he heard his children had died. Jacob did the same when he was told his son Joseph was dead. And David tore his clothes when King Saul died. Francy? Francy?" Francy was asleep in my arms.

But I was busy thinking. I thought of the basket with envelopes of money to help pay the funeral expenses, and of her mother not having any insurance and being left penniless. I made a decision. I would put my *pushka* money into an envelope and drop it into the basket. Gosh, I thought. I guess I'll never get finished saving for Philly's taillight.

14 Good News

At breakfast the next morning Arnie had a lot of questions about death and funerals.

"Mama, can I go with Leely after school to visit Carmine?"

"I don't think so, Arnie. You're too young."

"I'm the same age as Carmine, and he's not too young."

We laughed. But as usual, Evy was ready with an explanation. "Arnie, what Mama means is that you're too young to be exposed to an environment of death. Carmine has no choice; it's his father that died. He has to be there."

"How about Leely? Mama let her go."

"Leely is older than you. She can handle it better," Mama answered.

Arnie pouted and kicked his foot.

Downstairs we said goodbye. Francy insisted on walking home by herself. We crossed the street to the schoolyard. It was buzzing with news of Mr. Piccolo's death. Millie had told Adeline and Irene that

Francy had slept over that night. I wasn't a bit surprised. With Millie's apartment directly across from ours, and the way her mother kept their door open most of the time, she knew almost everything that went on in my house. I was approached by everybody who knew Francy. Having everyone come to me for information made me feel important. I answered as many questions as I could, except about her mother being left penniless. I knew that if it had been me, I wouldn't want anyone to know that my family was poor. Anyway, it wasn't anybody's business.

All morning my mind was on how I was going to put my money into the basket. I decided not to sign the envelope; I didn't want to embarrass Mrs. Piccolo.

At lunchtime I told Mama and Papa what I planned to do with the taillight money. They didn't tell me not to do it, but they didn't encourage me either.

Mama sighed. "It's like a sack with a hole at the bottom—it just can't get filled up. My darling child, that's a big sacrifice to make. Do you want to start saving for the taillight from the beginning? Again? All you need is—what? Ten cents more?"

"I know, and I'm feeling disappointed. Very disappointed. But I thought a lot about it last night, and I weighed which feelings were stronger—the bad because I'll have to start saving all over again, or the good because I'll be helping them. The good won!"

"Don't do it, Leely! Don't do it!" Arnie cried out. "I gave you my own penny to help you save, and now you're gonna give it away?"

I looked at Arnie and felt guilty about his penny. I knew it meant a lot to him to help me. I let out a deep sympathetic breath and was about to hug him when a voice behind Papa said, "Good afternoon!" Rabbi Goldstein stood smiling.

"I'm glad you're here, Leely. I came to talk to your parents about your bat mitzvah. It took an awful lot of hard work to convince all the committees, but I finally got their approval. *Mazel tov,* Leely! You will be the first girl in this synagogue—I'll venture to say in this neighborhood—to become a bat mitzvah."

He extended his hand to me. I stood up and shook it. Papa was so happy, he smiled like a pumpkin.

Mama kissed me. "*Nu,* you wanted a bat mitzvah; now you got it. As if you don't have enough to do without it."

"So that's all there is to it? I can become a bat mitzvah? When?"

Rabbi Goldstein laughed. "Wait a minute, Leely. That's not all there is to it. There's a lot of preparing to do. I'll need you to come in after school today. We'll go over what you already know and discuss what you still have to learn, and that will determine the date."

"Rabbi Goldstein"—I twisted my hair and shifted from one foot to the other— "something happened since I spoke with you. I'm not going to be able to start my lessons."

The rabbi's face turned white. His eyes opened wide. "Leely, don't tell me, after all I went through that you—"

"No, no! Rabbi, I want it, I want it, but not right now. My best friend, Francy, her father died and her mother is left penniless. So I'm giving them all the money I saved to buy Philly Bronson a taillight. Now I have to start working twice as hard to save the money again, and I won't have time to begin my bat mitzvah lessons until after I have saved all the money I need for the taillight."

Rabbi Goldstein pulled on his ear and nodded. I could see he was trying to follow everything I said, but his squinting eyes showed he was having trouble. Speaking in Yiddish, Papa explained to him as simply as he could how hard I worked, how my *pushka* got stolen, and that now I was giving my money away. He ended with, "What can I tell you, Rabbi? She's a complicated child."

Rabbi Goldstein looked at me and combed his short-trimmed beard with his fingers. "So you'd rather give your money to charity and save all over again than start your bat mitzvah lessons?"

"I just don't know how many weeks it will take to save up sixty cents again."

"You know, Leely, charity is one of the most important commandments in the Torah. I think it's wonderful that you are practicing this *mitzvah* at such an early age. I really don't think it will take you too long to earn the money again."

I sighed. "I don't know, Rabbi. It's taken weeks and weeks already."

"God's miracles travel many paths, Leely. God will find a way to show approval of your good deeds. In the meantime, I'd still like you to come in this afternoon to talk. Mr. Dorman, will you be able to come with her?"

"Absolutely!" Papa pushed his chest out. "It will be my pleasure!"

The rabbi left. Papa spread his arms out wide to receive me. "So we're going to have a bat mitzvah in our family!" He almost crushed me with joy.

"But Dad, before we go to the rabbi's after school I have to drop off the envelope at Francy's. Okay?"

Luckily, when I got to Francy's house no one was in the living room, and I was able to slide the unsigned envelope into the bottom of the basket unseen. The right wall was covered with wreaths and vases of all kinds of flowers. I had never seen so many flowers at one time in my life, and the aroma in the room was heavy and sweet. The coffin was in the middle of all the beautiful flowers. I closed my eyes, then opened them to slits. Slowly I glanced from the side of my eyes at the open casket. I froze and held my breath. Mr. Piccolo looked alive. He had makeup on his face. I guessed they must have put it on to hide the dead look. He lay there as though asleep. He was there, and yet I knew he wasn't there at all. My heart pounded, and I ran out.

I found Francy in her bedroom sewing a hem. "I can't stay long, Francy. I have to go to see the rabbi. He said I can become a bat mitzvah, but he has to test me first."

"That's wonderful, Leely! But, you have to explain a bat mitzvah to me. I don't understand it."

"I will after I see him. Then I'll know more." We were sitting on Francy's bed. "It's quiet in your house today. Not as many people."

"Yeah, they're all cried out for now. Come tonight. More people will come, and the crying will start all over again."

"When's the funeral?"

"Sunday. Wanna come?"

I had been afraid Francy would ask me. My heartbeat picked up speed. "Francy, I've never been to a funeral or a cemetery. I feel uncomfortable about going. Will you be angry with me if I say no?"

"Oh, no! I won't be angry. I've never been to a cemetery before either, but I did go to my Uncle Giuseppi's funeral. There was a lot of crying there, too, I didn't like it much either, so I understand."

"Thank you!" I hugged Francy. "I've got to go now. Don't forget to come and sleep over again tonight."

"Okay, if I have to, I will. Wait, I'll walk to the door with you."

We passed by the kitchen. Mrs. Piccolo sat at the table having coffee and pastries with relatives I had seen the day before. "Girls, come have some milk and cake. This is Francy's best friend." She said something in Italian, and they all looked up at me and smiled.

"Thanks, Mrs. Piccolo, I'll have a cookie." On the tray of goodies covered with chocolate and whipped cream one pastry in particular caught my eye. "Oooh, may I have one of those? It looks so good." I pointed to a small cigar-shaped pastry filled with a white cream and topped with powdered sugar.

"*Cannoli!*" the relatives exclaimed, smiling approval. They watched my reaction as I took a bite. The flaky crust melted with the sweet, creamy filling. I closed my eyes as I rolled the pastry over my tongue. Then my taste buds responded. "Mmmmmm." I opened my eyes—they widened and almost popped. "This is so-o-o good!" Francy's relatives looked at me, nodding and smiling with gratification.

"Leely, do the Jewish people make anything like this?"

"No, nothing." I bent over the pastry platter and examined all the pastry. I saw a piece that resembled *mondelbrot*. "My mother makes something like this. We call it *mondelbrot*."

"I tasted it, Mama. It's good," Francy hastened to add.

"Does it have a licorice flavor?" one of the relatives asked.

"No, almond. And sometimes she adds different dried fruits—raisins, dates, apricots ,and whatever."

"Mm. Sounds really good," Francy's Aunt Angie remarked.

I was ready to leave. I looked at Mrs. Piccolo. Her usually pink complexion was grayish, her eyes were red, and her face looked tired and sad. I don't know how I got there, but I found myself with my arms around her. She hugged me back. I tried to control a sob. She patted my back, and I kissed her on the cheek. I couldn't find the right words, so I said nothing and turned to leave for Papa's store. At the door I looked back and said, "But you should taste my mother's *strudel*. It's delicious!"

"The funeral is Sunday," I told Papa as we walked to the synagogue, my arm linked with his. "Do you think I should go to keep Francy company?"

"Francy won't be missing company. I'm sure there will be plenty of people."

We walked through the sanctuary and passed the section where the classrooms were. The bar mitzvah class was having a lesson. Some of the boys looked up as we passed, and they waved. I didn't see Philly. I wondered why.

Moish called to me as we passed. "Are you gonna have a bat mitzvah, Leely?" I smiled and nodded my head.

"Wow!" Moish shouted. "Leely is going to be a girl bar mitzvah!"

"No kidding?" Red was surprised. The teacher wasn't; he must have known, because he was all smiles.

"You know all those boys?" Papa asked as we walked on to the rabbi's office.

"Most of them, not all."

"So many boyfriends you got?"

"No, Dad, I only have one."

"Oh! So who's the one boyfriend?"

Just then we passed the cantor's office. The door was open. There was Philly slumped over a book, chanting. The cantor greeted Papa with a nod and a "Good afternoon."

Philly looked up. He smiled. "Hey, Leely, did you get the bat mitzvah?"

I felt my face turn red. "Yeah, I got it."

"Great! When?"

"I'm on my way to the rabbi now to find out." I waved goodbye and walked on.

Papa looked at me and nodded his head. "Aha! *Nu*, so now I know who the boyfriend is. Right?"

I tightened my grip on Papa's arm and twisted a strand of hair.

Rabbi Goldstein was expecting us. He had some books open on his desk, and he used them to test me. He asked a lot of questions about holidays, the Ten Commandments, how the Torah came to be, and about Abraham, Isaac, Jacob, Moses, and other biblical figures.

"Okay! Leely, if you concentrate on learning to chant the *trope* and the prayers, you should be able to become a bat mitzvah in six months. I'll give you two weeks to save your money for the taillight, and then you have to start studying with the cantor." The rabbi opened his calendar book to look for a date.

"Rabbi, don't I have to be thirteen to become a bat mitzvah? I'm only going to be twelve in February."

"No, you don't. Girls mature earlier than boys. And you have already proven you can handle responsibility."

Papa sat back in his seat, smiling. "She should have been a boy, huh, Rabbi?"

"No!" the rabbi answered. "Be proud of how much she has accomplished as a girl. A boy *has* to do this; she *wants* to do it. That's saying a lot for her as an individual."

"You're right! I'm more proud of her because she's a girl."

"Okay, here it is." Rabbi Goldstein wrote as he spoke. "The date is May 7, 1938. Saturday morning on the seventh of May you will become a bat mitzvah. You will say the prayers and read the *Haftarah*. In addition, you will prepare a speech on that week's Torah portion, Kedoshim." The rabbi's white teeth shone brightly in contrast to his dark beard. "Good luck!"

15 *The Miracle*

It was quiet. In fact, it was very quiet for a Sunday afternoon. There were no customers in the drugstore and no children playing outside. Maybe because it was the first real cold day, or because Sunday was a movie day. Most of my friends had gone to the movies to see Nelson Eddie and Jeanette MacDonald in *Naughty Marietta*. I could have gone with them. Papa had given me ten cents. But it was important for me to stay and earn money. Sunday was the busiest day for phone calls in the drugstore. I already had seventeen cents in my pocket—ten cents for the movies I didn't see and the rest from tips. Not bad!

I sat in the wooden phone booth reading a library book, *Anne of Green Gables*. I heard somebody go into the next booth. He made many calls and inserted a lot of change. I could hear the coins clink as his change dropped. I looked at the phone in front of me and, for no particular reason, stuck my finger into the coin box. I felt a cold metallic hollow and slid my finger out. With it came two coins, a nickel and a dime. I stared at the coins. What a surprise! My heart raced.

"Gosh!" I whispered to myself. "Fifteen cents!" My mind did a quick tally. I now have thirty two-cents. I calculated. And all in one day! But I don't really have it; it belongs to somebody who forgot to take their change out of the coin box. But who?

My eyes moved from side to side as though someone were watching me. My mind spun like a toy top: I can keep it! I found it! But what if the person comes back for it? Then I must return it. I'll just have to wait and see.

"It's a miracle," I said out loud. Then I thought, Aha! This is what the rabbi meant. What was it he had said? "God's miracles travel many paths." Is this a path?

Suddenly, in the midst of my thoughts, the phone rang, and I leapt from the seat, startled. It rang a second time. I held one hand against my chest and took a deep breath as I reached for the phone.

"Hello, drugstore."

"Hello!" said a man's voice with a heavy Yiddish accent. "Could you call Mrs. Nemoff from 610 Maple Street? Second floor back. It's a 'mergency! You know maybe where that is?"

"Yes, I know. She's my neighbor. Hold on and I'll go get her."

"Don't go. Run! It's a 'mergency! Tell her to hurry. It's a 'mergency."

"Okay, I'm running. Hold!" I dashed to the building I lived in. Panting as I ran up the steps, I leaned on the frame of Mrs. Nemoff's door and banged. Mrs. Nemoff usually kept her door open so she could

161

see who was going and coming. That day it was closed. I shouted as I banged, "Mrs. Nemoff! Telephone call for you in the drugstore!"

Mrs. Nemoff opened the door. "Who's calling me, you know?"

"No! He didn't say, but he said it's an emergency and you should hurry."

"A 'mergency? *Vey is mir!* What kind of 'mergency?" Mrs. Nemoff ran for her coat.

Mr. Nemoff, a slightly built man with glasses and a thin mustache, came to the door holding Beebe in his arms. "Was it a man or a woman?"

"A man. He had a shrieking voice."

"Oh, yeah? That's her brother!" He turned back to his house.

Well, no tip here. This was a free run, I thought as I went into my house to tell Mama about the money I had found. "Look, Mother! I've already got thirty-two cents." I held the money out for Mama to see.

"How come so much so fast?"

I explained about the coin box. "It's mine, isn't it? I don't know who it belongs to, so I can't return it. Right?"

"I guess right."

"Do you think it's God's miracle, like the rabbi said?"

Mama's eyes widened. "Miracles I don't know from, Leely. God doesn't do miracles so fast. If you got the whole amount of money in one day, maybe you can call it a miracle."

As I pondered that thought Mrs. Nemoff returned from her phone call still hollering, only this time it was louder. "*A klug is mir!* Woe is me! Sammy, Mama is in the hospital! A heart attack! We have to go right away." I watched from our foyer as she ran around in circles pulling on her hair.

Mama, hearing Mrs. Nemoff's screams, went to the door. I followed behind.

"*Oy,* Mrs. Dorman, *a klug is mir.*" Mrs. Nemoff wrung her hands. "My mama had a heart attack, she's dying! Leely, babysit for me for a few minutes until my girls come home. Millie and Rosie will be home soon; they went to the movies. Beebe is sick. She has a fever. I can't take her out in the cold."

My heart sank. I wasn't prepared to do this favor. "Gee, Mrs. Nemoff I purposely didn't go to the movies with Millie so I could get tips for calling people to the phone. And Millie left only a little while ago. She won't be home for two or three hours." I twisted my hair around my finger. I was in a dilemma. I felt it wasn't right to refuse Mrs. Nemoff in a time of need, but I also knew that if I stayed with Beebe it meant I wouldn't be able to make any more money that day. And Sunday, the best day for phone calls.

My disappointment must have shown on my face because Mrs. Nemoff said, "I'll pay you, I'll pay you! How much do you get for babysitting?"

"Ten cents an hour."

"*What? Ten cents?* That's too much! You think I'm made of money? Money doesn't grow on trees, you know. Who pays you so much money?"

"Mrs. Garcia. She pays me ten cents an hour, and if she's a little late, she gives me a tip."

Mrs. Nemoff thought for a moment. "I'll give you twenty cents, that's all!" she said as she ran back into her house. I marched behind Mrs. Nemoff and looked back at Mama.

"The miracle," I whispered over my shoulder. Mama shook her head, trying to hide a smile. She waved a threatening finger at me, but in a kindly way.

"Sammy, give Leely twenty cents," Mrs. Nemoff screeched as she ran to get her things together. Mr. Nemoff gave me a quarter from his pocket. He smiled and put his finger to his lips.

Mrs. Nemoff continued shouting orders. "Give Beebe juice and give her a nap. She has a fever. Take her to the toilet—I'm training her. You know where everything is, right? So I'm leaving." She went thumping down the steps, her husband at her heels plying her with questions in his soft voice.

Mrs. Nemoff continued ranting, "*Oy!* We have to hurry to the hospital. *Oy, vey is mir!*" Her voice trailed away outside the front hall door, and I was left in her foyer, looking down at Beebe with her red face and running nose.

I was happy with the quarter. I knew I could never make as much in tips for the next two hours. Mama was still standing in the doorway. She came up to feel Beebe's forehead. "She's warm. I hope you don't catch from her anything."

I followed behind Mama, leading Beebe by the hand as I walked back into our house. "So, Mother, I made fifty-seven cents in one day. I need sixty. If I make the whole amount today, like you said, will it be a miracle?"

"So much money you made in one day?" Mama's eyes were doing some thinking; they were also smiling. "Looks like you'll be able to start your bat mitzvah lessons sooner than you or the rabbi thought. *Nu,* seems God's hands work in many ways."

I was satisfied that it was a miracle. "I'd better put the money away." I went to get Beebe, who was running after Malkah, calling, "Kitty, kitty," and took her into the bedroom with me. I counted fifty-seven cents. I knotted the money in the handkerchief, my *kenippel,* and hid it again in the back of my drawer. "Come back to your house, Beebe. We'll play with your toys."

I gave Beebe some orange juice I found in a can in the refrigerator and noticed she had wet her pants. "Let's get you some dry panties." Beebe ran ahead to where her panties were kept. There were two on the hot radiator, yellow, dry, stiff, and smelling awful from urine. I wrinkled my nose and changed Beebe into a dry pair. I started to put the wet panties on the radiator, but I couldn't—it hit me bad. I pinched my nose, carried the wet pants between two fingers to the bathroom, and dropped them into the sink. Then I sat on the floor and rolled the ball to Beebe. Soon Beebe got bored, and I looked in the toy box for something else to play with.

"How about blocks? Do you want to build a house with blocks?"

Beebe nodded. "Box, box." She took a block from my hand. I searched for more blocks in the toy box. There were all kinds of household things mixed in with her toys: spoons, lids from jars, pans, candles, wooden mixing spoons, used-up thread spools, and so on. I pushed them aside to get to the blocks at the bottom.

"We're gonna build a house, okay?"

"'Kay."

We built four sides, leaving small spaces for windows and a larger space for the door. "Now what can we use for a door?" I rummaged for something rectangular and came out with a blue charity box. Every Jewish house had a blue charity box. I placed the unpainted back of the box toward the outside. The silver metal glared at me. There were letters scratched onto the metal, L-E-E-L-Y. I had scratched them on myself.

My heart dropped to my stomach. "Hah!" I sucked in my breath and grabbed my pounding chest. I exhaled a raspy cry. "Oh, my God! My missing *pushka!*" I looked at Beebe and asked her, "How did it get here?" Beebe stared at me with her big innocent eyes, not understanding. For a while I was stuck to the floor. I couldn't move, I couldn't speak, and I could scarcely breathe.

Then I picked up Beebe and carried her to her crib. "Time for a nap, Beebe." I covered her and left. In the living room I sat in the large club chair and stared at the empty *pushka* in my hands. The name, Leely, was clearly scratched in the metal. How could they not have seen it? I tried to imagine who would have removed it from the wall. I knew well who was often in my room, but I just couldn't believe it. It was Millie! And all this time I had thought it was Adeline. I felt guilty—terribly guilty for thinking badly of Adeline. Pained and baffled, I started to cry.

Once Beebe fell asleep I went into my house holding my *pushka* close to my still-racing heart. Mama was ironing in the dining room.

Papa had just come home from the store. With tears running down my cheeks I held out the box for them to see. At first there was no response; they just stared and stared at the *pushka.*

"Where did you find it?" Mama asked.

"In Beebe's toy chest."

"Beebe's toy chest?" they said together.

Sobbing, I nodded my head. Mama and Papa were so stunned, they couldn't say a word. They looked at each other and shook their heads in disbelief. Then Mama took me in her arms, which made me cry all the more.

"I can't understand how Millie could do it. We're good friends. Why? Why would she do such a thing?"

Mama sighed. "Who knows why people do dishonest things? I don't know."

Papa said, "When things like this happen to you, when you feel the pain you're feeling now, it makes you want to strengthen your own honesty that much more. And also to be more careful who you choose to be friends with."

"But Papa"—I always slipped from Dad to Papa when I was emotional—"I did just that. I stayed away from Adeline because I thought she took the money. I knew she took extra money from her father's cash register, and I was afraid to trust her. I was careful, only with the wrong friend."

Mama and Papa nodded in agreement. "I can't be friends with Millie anymore. She knew how important that money was to me. She knew I was hurt, and she didn't care. *I hate her!*" I stamped my foot.

"I won't be friends with her, even though her mother is your customer."

"Leely, *mamele*," Papa said, "nobody is forcing you to be friends with anyone you don't like. We trust you to do the right thing."

"So what will you say to Millie?" Mama asked.

"I don't know yet. I'm going back to think about it before she comes home."

I returned to the Nemoff apartment and sat in the living room, planning what to say to Millie. I would tell her how heartless she was to let me suffer. That she was dishonest. A thief! I would leave out nothing. I would pour out everything that was on my chest. I memorized sentence after sentence.

When Millie and Rosie returned they found me in the bathroom with Beebe. I had rushed her in when she woke up so I wouldn't have to change her again.

"What're you doing here?" Millie asked. "Where are my parents?"

"Your mother had an emergency. Your grandmother is in the hospital with a heart attack, so I'm babysitting. Now you can take over, and I'll go back to work before it gets too dark."

"Is my grandmother very sick?" Millie's eyes flooded.

"I don't know how sick, but sick enough to be taken to the hospital."

Millie bit her lip, and Rosie started to cry. "Is she going to die?" Rosie asked.

"I don't know, but if she's in the hospital, I suppose they'll take good care of her." I stood staunch for a moment and readied myself to tell Millie all the things I planned to say to her. I held up the *pushka*. "I found my *pushka* in Beebe's toy box," I said in a quavering voice as I stared hard at Millie. I shook the box to show Millie it was empty. My mouth tightened, and nothing more came out.

Millie's face turned white, then it turned red. Her mouth opened, but she didn't say anything either. I felt myself ready to explode into tears and ran out of her house.

I stood in our kitchen, angry with myself. Mama came in and waited for me to speak. "I planned a bunch of things to say to her, Mama, and all I said was that I found my *pushka* in Beebe's toy box." I threw my arms up in the air, annoyed with myself.

"Less is more," Papa said from the kitchen doorway.

"I told her about her grandmother. She cried. I guess I felt sorry for her."

"Silent words are golden words," Mama said, kissing me on my forehead. "Your message was stronger this way."

"I hope you're right, because she didn't say anything."

"Of course not! What could she say? 'Yes, I took it?'"

I sniffled. "I'm going back to the phone calls."

Papa shouted, "*Enough! Enough* already. Don't go to the drugstore. I'll give you what money you still need. You worked plenty hard and saved for three taillights already." Papa kissed me on my cheek. "Enough with the phone calls!"

Mama said, "*Nu,* Jacob, the child finally built for you enough character from all this bike riding, and black and blue marks, and muscle pains, and heartaches?"

Papa took me in his arms and gave me a big bear hug. "I don't think there is another girl in the whole world with so beautiful a character as my Leely." He held my cheeks with both hands and kissed me smack on the lips. "And we're the proudest parents in the world to have such a daughter."

Papa kissed away my pain. "Thanks, Dad!" I wiped my tears and gave them both a hug. "I'm going over to Francy's house. She should be back from her father's funeral by now."

Francy's house was noisy again. Loads of people were standing around, crying, eating. There was a lot of food on the table. It looked like a party, but a sad one. We went to Francy's bedroom. Her grandmother came out of her bedroom holding on to Mrs. Piccolo. "You all right, Grandma?" Francy patted the wrinkled cheek of the old woman, who nodded and muttered something in Italian.

It was quieter in Francy's bedroom. "You had to start saving from scratch again, didn't you, Leely? I know that was your money in the basket. And my mother does, too. I knew how much money you had in your *kenippel*, and that's exactly how much there was in the envelope."

"I had to do it, Francy. I felt I had to do something to help."

"I know. My mother and I spoke about it. It was a tremendous sacrifice you made. And I know how hard you've been working for the money. I'll tell you something, though: When the family opened the envelopes, yours was the most important one. Everybody commented on our how beautiful our friendship is. I was really proud, Leely. Proud that I have a friend who cares so much. Thanks! Thanks a lot!" Francy sobbed, then kissed me on my cheek.

"You're welcome. But don't worry I'll have all the money I need by the end of today."

"How come?"

"A miracle happened!"

"What? What kind of miracle?" Francy was all eyes and ears.

I told Francy what the rabbi had said, that God works miracles in different ways, and how all the money came to me in one day. She stared at me in awe of what I was saying.

"It *was* God's doing, Leely, because you're so kind. I definitely believe it was a miracle. Don't you?"

"Yup! It's a real miracle because the money came all in one day and almost all at one time." I stood up to take my coat off and felt the *pushka* in my pocket. I frowned. Should I or should I not tell Francy about it?

"What's the matter, Leely?" She looked concerned.

I returned her gaze and twisted my hair around my finger, thinking, Should I tell her? I never told anybody I thought Adeline stole my money, but Francy guessed. She shouldn't think that anymore. She's my best friend. I have to tell her.

"What? What's the matter?" Francy asked anxiously. I slipped the box out from my pocket. She gasped. Her hand flew to her mouth. She shook her head with questioning eyes and waited for me to explain.

I unfolded everything that had happened at Millie's house—where and how I found the *pushka*, how I never said all the things I planned to say, and how Millie reacted and said nothing. "I know it's wrong to talk about Millie, but this time I have the proof, and I can trust you not to tell anybody else because you're my best friend."

"You bet I am! Gosh! I can't believe she would do such a thing. And all the time you thought Adeline had stolen your money."

"I never said that, Francy."

"You didn't, but I could tell you believed it. I could see you were avoiding her whenever you could." Francy stared out her window, shaking her head. "I just don't understand how she could do it." After a few moments she pulled herself back with a start. "Anyway, with the miracle and all, you now have enough for a taillight, right?"

"I need three cents more. My father said I should go buy it—he'll give me the rest since I saved enough for three taillights. Wanna come with me?"

"You bet!"

"I'll wait until you're finished mourning, then we'll go together."

Francy jumped off the bed. "I'd better get back to the family." She took my hand and led me out. "Ask Adeline, too, Leely. You owe her that for thinking she stole your money."

16 *Finally*

I invited Adeline to join us for the long-awaited event: buying the taillight.

"I want to go, too," Arnie said. "Carmine is going with Francy."

"Okay, okay, come on." I took Arnie's hand as we crossed the street. The bicycle store was on Utica Avenue. We had to walk up the hill to get there.

"Ask for a box, Leely, so you can wrap it like a special present," Adeline said.

"Good idea." Francy patted Adeline's back. "Philly waited a long time for it and never once asked when you were gonna give it to him, so he deserves"—she stretched each word—"an e-x-t-r-a s-p-e-c-i-a-l gift box."

My friends were happy for me. I could tell by the way they were all talking at once and rushing to get to the bike store. They were as eager as I was to get the light bought and into Philly's hands. They had suffered through it all with me.

The bicycle store was dim and dingy. There were different-size bikes in assorted colors. Some were new, some were old, and some were waiting to be fixed. All kinds of bicycle parts were strewn around—some loose, others in boxes on dusty shelves.

There was no one in the store. We waited for someone to appear. "Can I help you, young ladies?" We looked around to find where the voice had come from. It was from the dark corner of the store, where a man was sitting on the floor fixing a bike.

"I'd like to buy a taillight for a bike, please." I strained my eyes to focus on the man.

"Okay, I'm coming." The man stood up—and up and up. He was so very tall that he looked like he grew out of his hair. And he was all skin and bones—so skinny and flat-looking that his belly went inward and his pants looked as if they would drop if he so much as unbuckled his belt. His hair and clothes were dark gray, and he could easily have disappeared into the background of the dark store. Until he smiled. He had a beautiful smile, warm and friendly.

"What kind of taillight would you like?"

I looked at the girls. They all shrugged their shoulders. Arnie called out, "A big red one!"

The man smiled. "How much do you want to spend?"

"No more than sixty cents." The man nodded, went to a shelf on the side wall, and brought back two boxes. One had small lights about an inch and a half in diameter, and the other had two-inch taillights.

"Hey, look at these!" Adeline said. "He's got green ones, too."

"But Philly's is red," Francy commented.

"Yeah, Philly's is red," Carmine echoed.

"How do you know?" Arnie asked.

"I know because it's broken and I always look at it when he rides by. And it's this size." Carmine pulled out a two-inch light from the box and held it up.

I tapped Carmine on the head. "You're right, it is that size."

"I like the green one best," Irene said.

"The green is nice, but I think I'd better stick to the same color. How much is the larger one, Mister?"

"Fifty cents."

"Fifty cents? Wow! That'll leave me with ten cents over." I widened my eyes as I thought. "Do they come larger?"

"Yes, I've got a three-inch taillight, too." He walked back to the shelf.

"Boy!" I said, rubbing my hands together. "Wouldn't it be great if I could get Philly a light bigger than the one I broke?" The girls were all smiles.

The man brought me a larger light with more facets, and it was a richer shade of red. "Oh!" I was delighted. "This is so bee-yoo-tee-ful! I love it! I really like it a lot!"

"Does it sparkle?" Arnie asked. The man pulled a chain over the counter, and the light went on. Arnie grabbed the taillight from my hands and angled it in different directions. "Look how it sparkles! This is great!"

"How much is it?" I asked, going for my money.

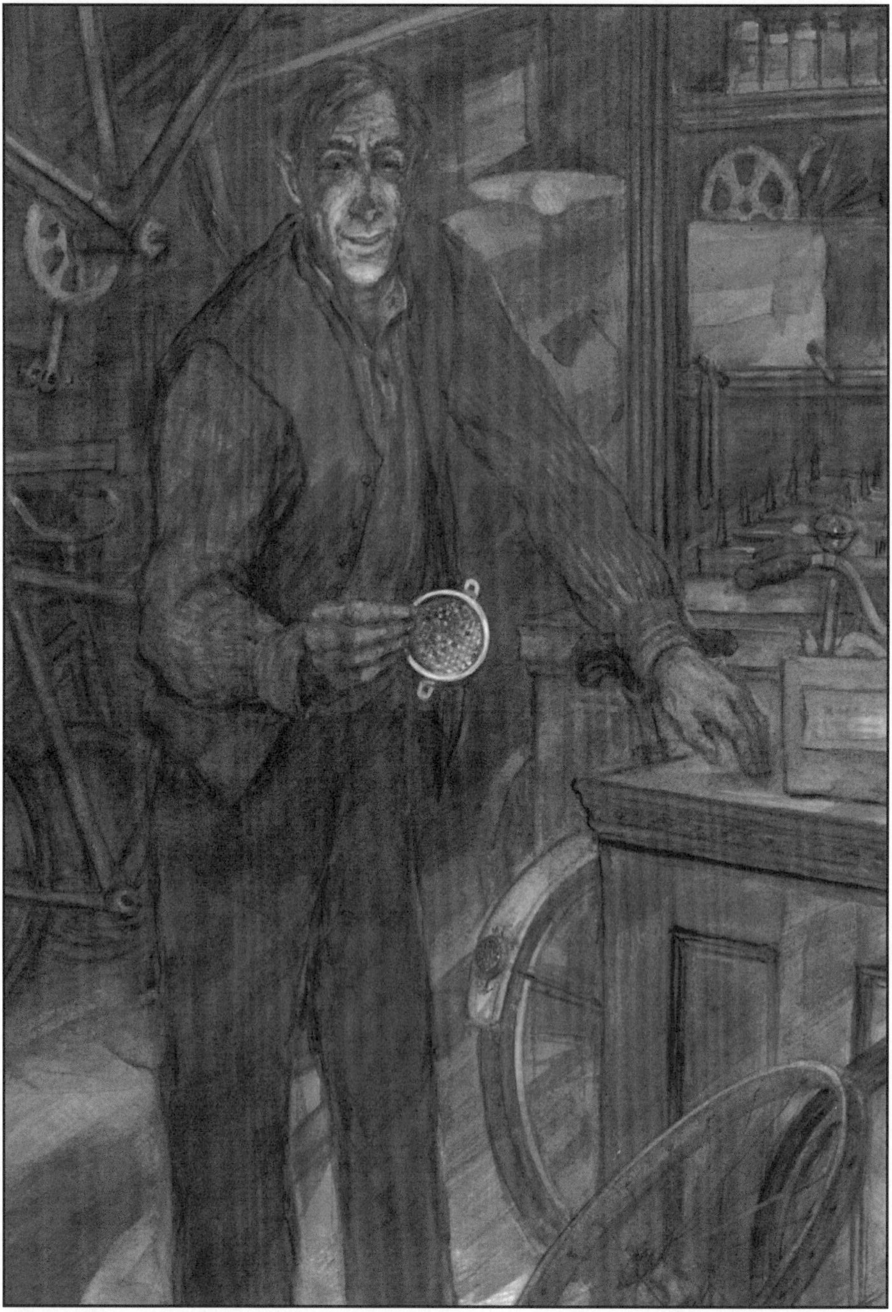

"Seventy-five cents."

"What?" My heart sank. "Oh, no! I don't have enough money—I only have sixty cents."

"Then take the smaller one," the man said. I looked back and forth from one taillight to the other. Each time I looked at the small light it seemed to shrink. My eyes stayed mostly on the larger one.

"I like this one better. Oh, gosh, what should I do? This one is really super! Isn't it, girls?" They nodded but had worried expressions on their faces. I ran my fingers over the facets of the red glass as I held it in the palm of my hand. "No! I can't take the smaller one. Now that I saw the larger light, I must get it. It'll make Philly very happy." I sighed deeply. "I'm sorry, mister. Thank you very much. I'll be back in a few days." I turned to leave. "Let's go!" Nobody followed me.

Arnie cried, "Aw, come on, Leely, take the smaller one."

"Yeah, come on, Leely," Carmine echoed.

"Leely," Francy said, "take what you can afford, or you'll never get the taillight. If you're going to be piggish, it'll take you forever, and Philly will get tired of waiting. He'll buy it himself."

Arnie and Carmine were whining, "Take the small one already. It's nice, too." They pulled on my coat to keep me from leaving, but my mind was made up. I was going back to deliver more orders.

My friends lagged behind me with disappointed frowns on their faces. Except for Adeline; she was still standing at the counter wiggling in funny positions. Her hand was way down in her coat pocket, and she was twisting from side to side.

"Adeline, come on!" I called. "What in the world are you doing?"

"I knew I had some money in my pocket, but I found a hole instead. The money must have fallen out."

"Let me see." Francy ran back and thrust her hand into Adeline's pocket.

I cried, "Adeline, don't bother. Thanks anyway, but I don't want to take your candy money. I'll just deliver more orders and run some more phone calls. Don't worry. I'll come back for it. Come on, let's go!"

Francy and Adeline ignored me. "This isn't a hole, Adeline, it's a torn seam. Take the coat off—I'll find it." Francy knew just how to probe the hemline.

"Here they are. I can feel them." She stuck her hand into the torn pocket and slid it behind the lining. "I've got them!" Francy withdrew her hand, bringing out two nickels and a penny. She smiled broadly and handed the money to Adeline.

Adeline said, "Here, Leely, take this money and get the large light."

"No, I can't do that! I don't want to take your money—it's not right."

"It's right if I want you to take it. It's God's way of working miracles. Just like the rabbi said. Please take it. As far as I knew, I had lost the money. I didn't even know it was in the hem of my coat." Adeline forced the money into my hand and pushed me toward the counter.

"I'll pay you back, then, okay?"

"No, it's not okay. I want to give you the money. I feel good helping you. Please!"

I wanted to get the taillight all by myself. I didn't want any help from anyone else. But I also knew how Adeline felt. It had to be the same as when I had put my money into Mrs. Piccolo's funeral basket. And that was the most wonderful feeling of sharing I had ever experienced.

"Okay. Thanks! You're a good friend, Adeline." I held my hand out to the man with all the money in it. "I've got seventy-one cents, mister. That's all I've got." Our eyes were on this tall, skinny man behind the counter who had been watching and listening to what we were doing all this time. No one spoke. Our pleading eyes did all the speaking.

The storekeeper looked at the money in my hand and then at our faces. He flashed his teeth. "Sold!" he said and he took the money. We clapped our hands and hugged one oather. Arnie and Carmine punched each other playfully on the arms.

"Thanks a whole bunch, Adeline!" The girls said. They were grateful, too.

"You're welcome." We stood there beaming with satisfaction. The man put the taillight into a bag.

Francy asked, "Mister, would you have a small box?"

"A box?" The man looked puzzled. "I don't sell boxes. I sell chains and pedals and bolts and bikes, but no boxes."

"I need a box so I can give it as a present. Maybe you have a box from your screws or bolts?" I pointed to the shelves. "Like those."

"A box," the man repeated as he looked around his store shelves. He brought his finger to the side of his forehead and nodded. He stepped through an open doorway at the back of the store and returned in a few moments, grinning. "This is perfect!" He held up a box about four inches square. "Isn't this perfect? My rubber washers come in these boxes."

I placed the light inside the box, and, to our delight, it fit. "Perfect!" we all exclaimed. We thanked the man and left.

Outside the store I stopped and took a deep breath. "Finally! I finally got the taillight. You know what, girls? I think this was one of the hardest things I ever had to do in my whole life, but I did it, finally!"

Arnie pulled at my sleeve. "Leely, this is the biggest light I ever saw in my whole life. I bet Philly will be proud to put it on his bike. What do you think, Carmine?"

"I think Philly is gonna love it. He'll ride around and around the block to show it off." Carmine made circles in the air.

"Yeah! He'll show it off, " Arnie nodded.

"Do you have wrapping paper, Leely?" Irene asked.

"Are you kidding?" I raised my eyebrows. "I don't have wrapping paper. Do you?" Everyone shook their head.

"We have to get wrapping paper and ribbon." Adeline said.

"Francy, you have a bunch of ribbons," Carmine said, "why don't you give Leely one?"

"Of course! Carmine is right. If I don't have the color you need, my mother can bring it from the factory."

"I can get the tissues that wrap the fruit and we can paste them right onto the box."

"Okay!" I shouted. "Let's go wrap the taillight!"

17 Wrapped and Ready

ADELINE'S MOTHER GAVE US YELLOW TISSUES FROM AN ORANGE crate. Her father found some green shredded cellophane among the apples. "Here," he said, "stuff this around the taillight. It'll look nice." We took the wrappings to Papa's white enamel table.

"It's some beauty!" Papa said as he examined the light. He pursed his lips as he always did when he thought something was unusually nice or good. "It's such a big one! How much did it cost?"

We all answered at one time, trying to explain how we got the "miracle" money in Adeline's coat. His eyes shifted from face to face, absorbing as best he could what we were telling him. In the end he got the gist of it and laughed.

Arnie said, "Twist it around, Papa. See how it sparkles in the light."

"So when will you give it to him?" Mama asked.

"As soon as Francy gets me a ribbon. I want to tie it with a pretty bow."

"So then you'll give it to him for Hanukkah? In a few days will be Hanukkah."

I hadn't thought about giving it to Philly for Hanukkah. I looked at my friends. "What do you think, should I wait for Hanukkah?"

Irene said with a wave of her hand, "Give it to him already. The poor guy has waited so long for it."

"It's only a few more days," Adeline said.

"Don't wait for Hanukkah, Leely! Give it to him right away!" Arnie bounced impatiently. He was eager to see the light on the bike.

"Yeah, don't wait," Carmine echoed Arnie.

Mama stood with her arms folded across her chest listening to us try to decide how and when I should give Philly the taillight.

Adeline offered her opinion. "I like the idea of giving it to him for Hanukkah. Somehow it sounds more—more—festive."

"I agree," Francy added. "It's like giving a Christmas present. It has more meaning than just giving it on an ordinary day."

We continued the discussion while we smoothed the yellow tissue papers out on the table. "Now we need glue to paste them on the box. Where are we going to get the glue?" Irene asked. Irene was the creative one.

"Upstairs in my house," Adeline said. Then she flew out of the market and returned in no time holding a jar of white school paste. Her eyes were beaming, and she was all smiles. "Guess what I thought of?"

"What?" we all asked.

"Why don't we have a Hanukkah party?"

"What's a Hanukkah party?" Francy asked.

"I don't really know," I answered. "We never actually had a party for Hanukkah. We just make potato *latkes*, light candles every night, and sing Hanukkah songs. And we get Hanukkah *gelt,* money, from my parents."

"And don't forget we play with the *dreidel*, too," Arnie said.

I thought about it, but not for long. I liked the idea. I looked to Mama, who was watching us wrap the box. "Mother, how would we make a Hanukkah party? What would we need?"

"Like you said, you make *latkes*, serve them with sour cream and applesauce, play *dreidel*, sing Hanukkah songs, and that's a Hanukkah party!"

Francy asked, "What are *latkes* and *dreidels*?"

Irene and Adeline rushed to answer. "*Latkes* are pancakes, and *dreidels* are spin tops. We play for nuts or candy. So what do you think?" Adeline was excited with her idea of a party. "You want to make potato pancakes?"

Francy said, "Yeah! Let's make them. What do we need?" Adeline's enthusiasm was rubbing off on Francy.

"Potatoes, eggs, matzoh meal or flour, and what else?" I looked at Mama.

She counted on her fingers as she continued listing the ingredients for me. "Salt, pepper, onions, oil—that's all!"

"We have to peel and grate a whole lot of potatoes. It's a lot of work. Are you sure you wanna do it?" I asked uncertainly.

"I don't mind the work. Especially if we work together," Francy said.

"Neither do I. It'll be a lot of fun, all of us cooking together." Irene brushed paste on the last piece of tissue paper and handed it to me. "What about sour cream and applesauce? I think we should chip in and share. Don't you?"

I pressed the tissue paper on the box and held it up for inspection. "It looks great!" Everyone agreed.

"Now all we need is the ribbon. Tell me what color you want. If I don't have it, my mother will bring it home tomorrow," Francy said.

"Purple. What do you think of purple on yellow tissue paper? Yucky or good?" I asked.

"I think it's bright and colorful," Adeline said. "It will dazzle Philly's eyes when you give it to him."

"Then purple it shall be!" I placed the yellow box on the table, and we all admired it with goofy-looking smiles on our faces. "So where are we gonna have the party?" We all shrugged our shoulders.

I called out to Mama, who was now at the far end of the counter. "Mother, can we have the party in our house?"

"And when would you have it?" she called back.

We looked at each other and we all said, "Saturday night."

"Saturday night," Arnie repeated.

"Saturday night! Saturday night!" Carmine's little voice sang out.

"Say, you guys, go outside and play. This party has nothing to do with you." I turned the two of them toward the door.

"Gee whiz! Can't I even get some *latkes*? Mama, can I get a *latke* at the Hanukkah party?"

"Don't be a pest, Arnie, go outside. I'll save you a pancake."

"Me, too?"

"You, too, Carmine. Go!"

"Mother, so how's Saturday night? Can we have it in our house?"

"Saturday night I have to be in the store with Papa. You can't have a party without a parent in the house." Our faces dropped.

"That's too bad," Adeline said. "My mother is in the store on Saturday night, too."

"My mother is home, but would you want to have the party in a Christian home? That doesn't make much sense." Francy laughed.

We laughed, too. "Don't be silly Francy. Even if we could have it in your house, we wouldn't. It's too soon after your father's—uh—funeral," I said, placing my arm around her.

We looked at Irene. "I don't know. I'd have to ask my mother."

We sat around the table trying to figure out how and when to have the party. As we made plans Evy and her friend Trudy came into the store. Trudy was pretty. She was petite. Her nose was small and thin and tilted up at the tip. She had high cheekbones and jet-black hair.

"Why do you all look so sullen? Didn't you get the taillight?" Evy asked.

"I did. And what's more, I got a bigger and better one."

"Really? Let's see it."

I held up the wrapped box. "It's in here."

"Oh! It's wrapped already. So we can't see it. How much bigger is it?"

"It's this big." I made a circle with my hands. "It's three inches in diameter, and it's beautiful."

"Did it cost more?" Trudy asked.

"Yes, it cost seventy-five cents," Francy answered for me. "And Adeline gave her the extra money, but we only paid seventy-one cents."

"How come?" Evy asked. We told the whole bicycle store story again.

"That was very nice of you, Adeline," Trudy said.

Evy fluffed her drooping curls. "Philly will probably be tickled pink to get a bigger and better taillight. When are you going to give it to him?"

"This weekend. For Hanukkah. We were just talking about making a Hanukkah party—"

"On Saturday night," Adeline interrupted.

Francy continued, "But your mother said we can't have it because she won't be able to be there. I guess she means as a chaperon."

Evy and Trudy looked at each other and smiled. "We'll be happy to chaperon for you, won't we, Trudy?"

"Absolutely!" Trudy replied.

"Would you? Gee, that would be great!" exclaimed Adeline.

"No it won't, either," I said. "Don't be in such a hurry to accept. Be careful, Adeline. My sister probably has something up her sleeve. This is gonna be our party, Evy, not yours."

"So who said it won't be your party? For goodness sakes! I'm only offering to do you a favor so you can have a party." It became quiet. Nobody spoke.

Finally Evy said, "Who were you having, anyway?"

"The four of us and four boys, right?" I asked my friends.

"How about Millie?" Trudy asked.

"Definitely not!" I stamped my foot. Although I had never told anyone why I was no longer friends with Millie, somehow they had found out all about it.

"She lives on our floor. She'll know you're having a party."

"Good! That'll be her punishment. I'm mad at her, and I don't want to talk about her anymore."

"Okay, okay." Evy put her hands up. "So you're going to have a lot of cooking to do. Don't you want us to help you?"

"No, thank you. We can manage." I raised my chin with a haughty fling.

"Trudy and I can help in the kitchen while you're playing *dreidel* or whatever. We can give you some reprieve." Evy held her finger up. "Watch this. Mother, if I stay at home and lend an eye while Leely and her friends have a party, could she have it Saturday night?"

"If you take care there shouldn't be any accidents or fire while they cook, and that everything is good and proper, and the neighbors don't complain—yes."

"See, do I know my mother?"

"Do I know my sister? Just why are you so good to me? What are you up to?"

"Nothing! I'm just trying to be nice, for crying out loud!"

Adeline said, "Leely, I don't mind if the two of them come. That way we can have the party. Otherwise we just don't have one."

Francy patted me on the back. "It's just the two of them. Let them come, Leely."

I folded my arms across my chest as I studied Evy's phony innocent face. "No sneaky surprises, Evy, I'm warning you."

"We're all chipping in with the food. I'm gonna see what I can bring." Adeline left to speak to her parents in the back of the market. She returned smiling openly. "My mother said she'll give us the potatoes and onions."

"Wow! All of it? Did you tell her we'll be ten people?" I asked.

"Yup!" Adeline started the ball rolling.

"Listen!" Francy jumped up from her seat. "We have a bushel of apples my Uncle Al brought from the produce market in Manhattan, where he works. I could make the applesauce."

Trudy said, "We have some decorations left over from my kid sister's birthday party. I could bring balloons and crepe paper streamers."

"Wonderful! That would really make it look festive." Irene was into "festive."

"I'll bring the sour cream and whatever else I can get," Irene offered.

"Then we'll supply the eggs, oil, and flour. Okay, Mother?"

Mama was ready to go home. She carried a pot of food she had cooked in the store for dinner. "Yes, it's okay. Make sure everyone brings a peeler and grater for the potatoes and onions or you'll never get finished. If it's not a kosher grater, they can't bring it."

"Uh-oh! That's me," Francy said. "My grater certainly isn't kosher."

Evy and Trudy were standing to the side whispering to each other. Trudy said, "Leely, would you like some holiday candy like sesame seed candies? Candies filled with fruits and jellies?"

"Sure, why not?"

"You know our friend Barbara? Her father owns an imported candy and nut store. She'd be able to get us some."

Evy said, "You could use them for prizes when you play *dreidel*. But I guess we'd have to ask her to join us if we want the candy."

"That's it!" I threw my hands up. "What did I tell you, girls? Be careful, she'll sneak something over on us. Now Evy wants to bring another girlfriend. Soon they'll be running the whole party their way."

"Don't worry, we won't run your party. If you don't want her to come, she won't," Evy said, waving her hand nonchalantly. But look at all the nice candy you'd be missing. It's up to you girls—whatever you say is fine." Evy turned away as if she couldn't care less, but I knew otherwise. She wanted her two best friends at the party. Francy and Adeline were nodding their heads for me to say yes. They wanted the candy.

I half closed my eyes suspiciously. I waved a finger at Evy. "Only if she brings the candy." I puffed out my cheeks and blew out a deep breath. "*And no boys!* Remember, none of your boyfriends can come to this party!"

18 Act of Repentance

It was Saturday afternoon. Evy and I were coming home from the library. Arnie darted up the cellar steps, bumping into us and pushing us off balance.

"Hey! What do you think you're doing?" I yelled, almost falling to the ground.

Arnie dashed to the streetlight pole in front of our house. Tapping it, he shouted, "One! Two! Three! You're still it and I'm still free!" Arnie was playing hide and seek with his friend Herbie.

We laughed and walked up the stairs. At Millie's door Evy nudged me and pointed. The Nemoffs' door was open.

I whispered, "This is the first time I've seen their door open since I told Millie I found my *pushka* in Beebe's toy box."

"Maybe it's because Mrs. Nemoff's mother is better, " Evy whispered back. "Remember they were going back and forth to the hospital. They thought Millie's grandmother was going to die."

I put my finger to my lips, and we tiptoed into our house, closing the door as quietly as possible.

"Millie probably heard about my Hanukkah party and is going to try to finagle her way into it. No way am I gonna let her come. I hate her!"

Papa was reading his newspaper in the dining room. He folded his paper and said, "*Nu*, it's time to get ready to open the store."

"Can we prepare for the party yet?" I asked as I hung up my coat.

"Soon. Wait another half hour," Mama said.

There was a knock on the door. Mama answered it. "Leely!" she called. "Millie wants to speak with you."

I looked at Evy. "See? What did I tell you? She wants to come to my party."

Evy followed me to the door. I stood in front of Millie with my arms folded. I said nothing. I felt mean, and I'm sure I looked it, too.

Millie was holding a white and green striped box with a fancy green bow. Looking at my firm face, she bit her lip. She handed me the box. "Happy Hanukkah!" she said in a voice scarcely above a whisper.

I shook my head and refused to take her present.

Then in a loud quavering voice she cried, "I didn't steal your *pushka!*"

She forced the box into my hands. "Open it!" And with tears flooding down her cheeks, she turned and ran back into her house, slamming the door behind her.

Stunned by her outburst, I stood looking at her closed door. Evy tapped me on the shoulder and drew me back into the house. "Well," she said with raised eyebrows and pursed lips, "I think Millie's feelings were hurt."

Mama, who had been watching, said, "*Nu,* of course Leely hurt her feelings. She just stood there staring at Millie—not saying one nice word. Nothing! What do you expect? Feelings shouldn't be hurt?"

My mouth dropped open. "Hey, wait a minute! What about me? Don't I have feelings, too? I was very, very hurt when I found my *pushka* in her house."

"I know. But Millie was apologizing. When a person tries to say she's sorry, you should be nice, not mean." Mama slipped into her coat to leave with Papa.

"So open the box and let's see what's in it," Evy said.

I looked down at the box in my hands and put it on the dining room table. "I don't want it!"

"Leely, this is her act of repentance. She's sorry. You can't give it back—so do like Millie said and open it already. I'm curious to see what it is," Evy said, placing the gift in my hands. "Go ahead, open it!"

I looked at Mama and Papa. They, too, were waiting impatiently to see what was in the box. Hesitating, I turned the box around and around in my hands.

"*Nu shoin!* Hurry up already!" Papa shouted. "How long are you going to play around with it? Until tomorrow? It's almost dark, and I have to go to work."

I unwrapped the box slowly. Inside was a pink piggy bank. There were white and blue flowers painted all over the pig, and it had a blue bow tied around its neck.

After a moment of silence Evy said, "It's pretty."

Papa said, "Pretty but not kosher." We laughed.

"Oh, look! There's a note at the bottom," Evy said.

I took out the note. "This is not Millie's handwriting," I commented. I read the note out loud.

> Dear Leely,
>
> I am so sorry to give you so much pain. Your money was not stolen. I took it off the wall for Beebe to play with and forgot about it. Please don't be mad at Millie. She didn't know anything. Here is back your 49 cents and a bank to save for good reasons all your life.
>
> Mrs. Nemoff

I shook the bank, and the money clinked. "Wow! Can you believe that? Her mother took it! Wow!"

Mama and Papa looked at each other and shook their heads. They didn't say anything. They just kept shaking their heads.

"How embarrassing for Millie," Evy said.

Mama placed her hand on my shoulder. "Only embarrassing? And her pain? What about her pain? She didn't suffer? Believe me, Leely, it was worse than your pain."

"What? I don't believe my ears! Worse than my pain? No way!"

Papa said, "To apologize for a parent is not an easy thing to do. So maybe you have something to think about, yes? Like what to do with Millie, maybe?" Papa walked out of the house.

Mama said, "You can start your party now. I'll take your little brother with me so he shouldn't get in your way. Evy, make sure everybody behaves."

I stood staring at Evy. My jaw dropped, my arms were open, and I was totally confused. "Were they trying to make me feel guilty or something?"

Evy twisted her mouth to the side and nodded. "I think so."

"Why? What did I do wrong? All of a sudden my pain doesn't count anymore? Millie has more pain than I do? Something is not fair here!"

Evy walked into the kitchen. I followed. "Well, like Dad said, you think about it." Evy opened the cabinet and took out a mixing bowl. "The only pain you suffered was to think you had your money stolen by a friend. Millie was accused even though she was innocent. Second, she was embarrassed because her mother took the *pushka*. Third, she was humiliated by having to do an act of repentance for her mother. Fourth, you refused to acknowledge her apology and demeaned her by being snooty!"

"Well, how was I supposed to know her mother took it? I don't have a crystal ball, you know. What else was I supposed to think?"

There was a knock on the door. I stayed back in the dining room while Evy answered the door. "Leely, it's for you."

I dragged my feet as I inched my way to the door. Mrs. Nemoff's fat body was occupying the doorway. She had one hand on the

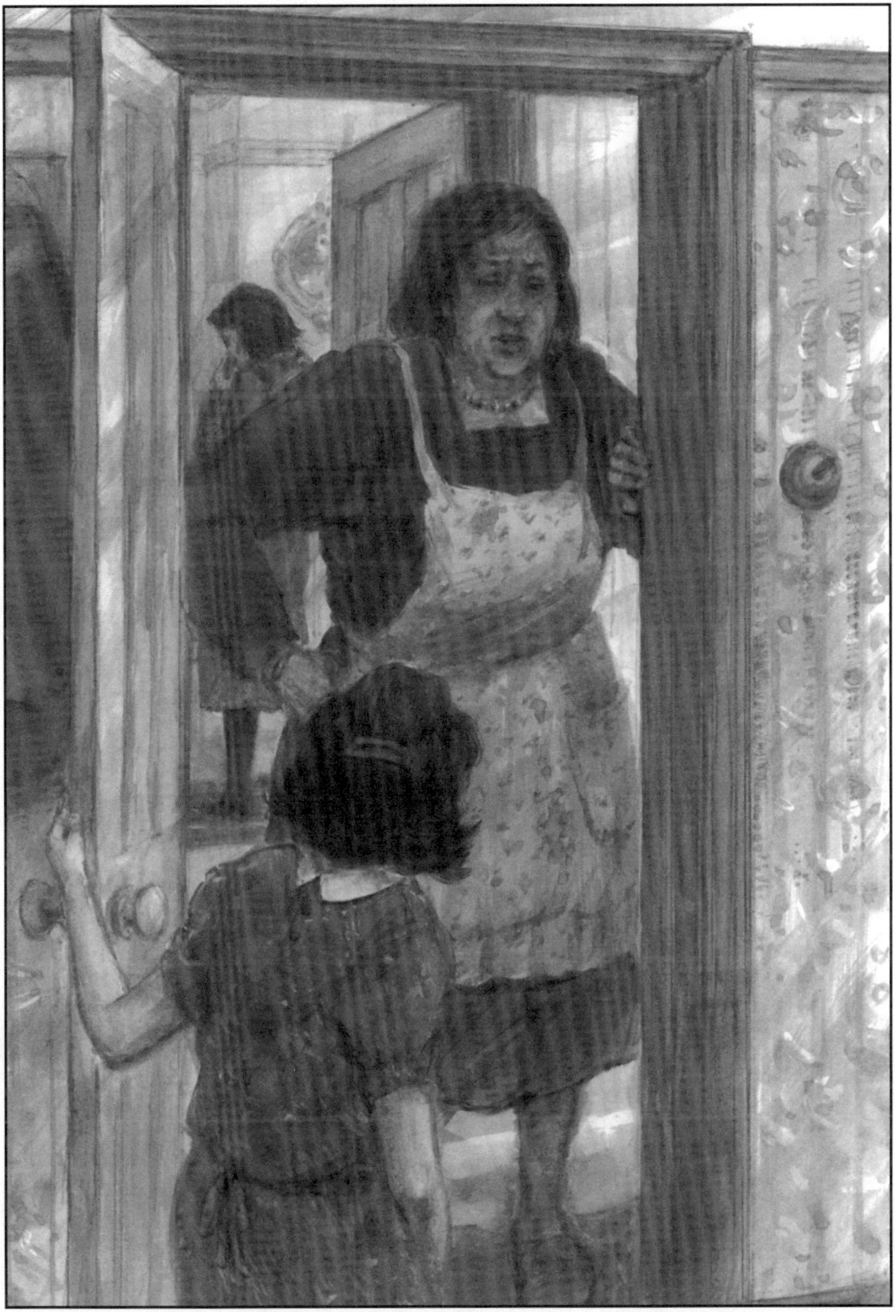

doorjamb and the other on her hip, forming a triangle of space between her and the door frame.

"Leely, did you open the box?" she asked. I nodded. "Did you read my note?" I nodded again. "So you know what happened?" I didn't nod. I just looked at Mrs. Nemoff.

"I was talking with your mama in the kitchen. But Beebe wanted to play with your box on the wall. She whined and *kvetched* and was driving me *meshugah*—crazy. I couldn't talk. So to keep her quiet I gave her the box for only a few minutes. I was going to put it back, but I walked out of the room and forgot. Millie didn't know from this nothing..."

Mrs. Nemoff kept rambling on, but I wasn't paying attention. Through the triangle of space her arm made I could see Millie standing at the far end of the foyer in her house. She was crying hard. My stomach turned with sympathy. I ducked under Mrs. Nemoff's elbow and walked up to Millie.

"I'm sorry, Millie," I said sincerely. "Now that I know what happened, you don't have to cry anymore." I put my arm around Millie's bouncing shoulders. Her sobbing only got louder. "I guess it was one big misunderstanding. I'm so sorry! But how could I know it was your mother who took my *pushka* off the wall. Look...you know I'm having a party tonight, right? So go wash your face and stop crying. Then you can come in and help us make *latkes*. Okay?"

"No, I can't come because they all think I stole your money."

"Okay, I'll tell you what. I'll explain to the girls exactly what happened before you come in. Then you won't have to feel embarrassed.

So stop crying now or your eyes will be red." I placed my hand on Millie's wet face and wiped it. I felt so sorry for her that the tears welled up in my eyes, too.

"Leely, I'm not angry with you." Millie's sobbing was subsiding slowly. "I really don't blame you for being mad at me. I guess I would think the same way if I were in your place."

"Well, I'm not mad at you anymore, either. Please stop crying. I really have to go and start the cooking for the party. The girls will be coming any minute."

I turned to leave and saw Mrs. Nemoff and Evy still standing in our doorway. Mrs. Nemoff's smile was almost as wide as she was. "Oh! And thanks! The piggy bank is adorable. I like it a whole lot!"

19 The Hanukkah Party

Evy and I were preparing the cooking utensils for the Hanukkah party. "This party is a good idea, Leely. It should be a lot of fun. All my friends loved the idea. They can't wait to see what Philly will say and do when you give him the light."

"All your friends?" I slammed the wooden chopping bowl down on the table. "Did you tell Philly's brother Yussy and all his friends that I'm giving Philly the taillight tonight? For Hanukkah?" The muscles on my face tightened.

"No! Of course not! I wouldn't spoil your surprise. I only told my girlfriends, and they were sworn to secrecy. Boy! You sure have me pegged for a monster. I *am* your sister, Leely, I am not out to hurt you. In fact, I'm very proud of you for your accomplishments. And my friends are, too. They know all the trouble you went through to get the sixty cents. They know your money was stolen, they know you gave all your money to Francy's family for the funeral, and they admire you for it." Evy's arms were flailing all over the kitchen as she spoke. "Why are you so distrustful of me, your sister, who loves you and is always supportive of you?"

"You want to know why I'm distrustful of you? Okay, I'll tell you. You're supportive of me only if you have nothing to lose by it. If your social life is affected, then you don't stand behind me. Even if it's your turn, you don't babysit Arnie if it means you can't go with your friends, and I have to drag him with me when I go with mine. You're a conniver, Evy, and you know it. You play innocent, then spring a surprise on me. And as far as your friends—well, they're always acting snobby and smug." I took the grater out of the cabinet and threw it into the bowl. "You act like big shots. Like you know everything and my friends and I know nothing. You treat us like babies."

"Well," Evy said, raising her eyebrows and shaking her head as she picked up Papa's newspapers, "I guess all big sisters feel they know more than their kid sister. It's only natural. So don't go getting all huffed up about it."

"Really! Well, just remember you were once my age. You weren't born fourteen, you know." I followed Evy into the dining room. "And just what do you think you're doing with those papers?" Evy was laying them on the dining room table.

"I'm spreading them out so there'll be more room for all of us to peel the potatoes at the same time."

"See, there you go again!" I shouted, pointing a finger at Evy. "You act like you know everything. Why don't you ask me if I want to do that? It is my party, you know."

"Okay, Your Highness." Evy bowed from the waist and curtsied. "Would you like to peel the potatoes and onions on the kitchen table, or would you prefer the larger dining room table, where everyone could peel at the same time? And would Your Highness like to prevent damage to Mother's table by spreading the newspapers for protection?"

I realized Evy was right this time, but I wasn't going to admit it. I stuck my nose into the air and said, "Your Highness okays your request to use newspapers for peeling potatoes." I swaggered back to the kitchen.

Coming in for the bowls, Evy asked, "When do you plan on giving Philly the taillight? At the beginning or at the end of the party?"

"I don't know. I haven't decided yet. Maybe in the middle."

"Why don't you give it to him right after everyone arrives? That way the evening could start on a happy note."

"Don't tell me what to do!" My cheeks filled up with angry air, but as I slowly exhaled I realized it was a good suggestion. But I wouldn't tell Evy I agreed with her.

In the midst of all this Adeline came in carrying two large bags filled with potatoes and onions. I ran to help her. "Good you came first," I said. "We can get started peeling."

"Hi, Addy!" Evy said, taking the other bag of potatoes. "Come on in. We're peeling in here."

Someone was slowly stomping up the steps. Francy, who had cooked the applesauce the day before, entered carrying two large jars.

"Hi, everybody!"

"Hi, Francy!"

My friends were considerate. Mama had said not to start before sundown, when the Sabbath would be over, and the girls arrived promptly just after dark.

"Come in here!" I hollered. "And put your coats on the bed." In the bedroom they saw the piggy bank Millie had given me.

"When did you get the piggy bank, Leely? It's pretty," Adeline said.

"Millie gave me a Hanukkah gift." I tried not to smile.

"*What?*" Francy, Irene, and Adeline sang out together.

"You heard right." I shook the bank so they could hear the money rattle. "Including the forty-nine cents that was missing with my *pushka*."

The three of them dropped on the bed. Their mouths dropped with them. I showed them Mrs. Nemoff's note. They gathered together and read it out loud—twice. When they finished all they could say was "Wow!"

Francy rocked from side to side with her hand on her cheek and said, "My God! It was her mother all the time!"

"Right! And Millie never even knew it had happened. Just before you arrived her mother came in to tell me how and why she took the *pushka* off the wall." I unfolded the whole story. They listened with their ears and eyes fixed on every word I said.

"I invited her to come to the party, but she said no. She's too embarrassed. So I told her I would speak to you first. That way you won't think badly of her when she comes in."

"Oh, for goodness sakes! I'll go get her." Francy stood up.

"I'll go with you." Adeline followed.

"Tell her to bring a grater and a peeler," I called after them.

They returned with Millie, who had washed her tears away and changed into a dress appropriate for the occasion (although this, too, was unhemmed). We went about preparing for the party as if nothing had ever happened between us.

Evy's friends arrived and pitched in immediately. "Hey, girls, look at this!" Trudy held up her grater. "All our graters look alike. How are we going to know whose grater is whose when we wash them?" We all checked out our four-sided metal graters with the handle on top and laughed.

Barbara suggested tying threads on them, each with her own color. I went for Mama's sewing box.

Evy emptied the bags of vegetables on the table. "Who's going to grate the onions?" she asked. No one answered.

"Adeline, they're your onions; you grate them," Irene said.

Adeline's mouth sprang open. "Wha—what? That's not fair. I was nice enough to bring them. You girls grate them." There was a wave of giggling around the table.

"Okay, okay, we'll all grate them." I distributed the onions evenly among the girls. We all peeled and grated and sniffled and laughed as we cried from the onions.

Much to my surprise, Evy's friends turned out to be very pleasant. I found them not to be stuck-up at all. I wondered if Evy had mentioned to them what I had said about them earlier. They told jokes and treated us as equals.

"What did the potato say to the onion?" Trudy asked as she peeled. Nobody knew the answer.

"We give up, what?" we all shouted.

"'I've got eyes only for you,'" Trudy said, and she scooped an eye bud out of her potato, which flew across the table.

Barbara came back with "What did the onion say to the potato?"

"What?"

"'If you get under my skin, I'll make you cry.'"

We laughed, and the jokes continued as we mixed the batter and fried the pancakes. A delicious aroma spread throughout the house. When the first batch came out of the skillet Francy said, "Oh, God! They smell so good." She licked her lips.

"Let's taste them," I said, not able to restrain myself. We all took a taste and immediately went into ecstasy. We closed our eyes and each slowly savored a mouthful. "Mm, mm, mm." Everyone moaned.

"Jeepers!" Evy said. "This tastes better than the mickies we ate at the bonfire." Smacking our lips, we all nodded in agreement.

Evy and her friends offered to fry the rest of the *latkes* while we decorated the dining room. Trudy had brought blue and white balloons and crepe paper streamers. We twisted the streamers across the ceiling with the balloons. We set the table with Francy's applesauce, Irene's sour cream and jam, plates and eating utensils. The Hanukkah menorah with orange candles was the finishing touch in the center of the table.

Millie brought a few bottles of soda from her house. The candy that Barbara had brought was set out on the buffet next to Philly's taillight. The large purple bow looked super on the yellow wrapping.

We all stepped back to examine the results. Irene said, "This room looks colorful and festive." She was satisfied; she had gotten the "festive" look she wanted.

In the kitchen Evy and her friends finished frying the *latkes*. They piled them on cookie sheets and placed them in the oven to keep them hot.

I separated some *latkes* for Mama, Papa, and Arnie. Also for Mrs. Piccolo and Carmine. "Boy, we'll have more than enough." I commented. "You brought a lot of potatoes, Adeline."

"I brought some also," Barbara remarked.

"And I added some of ours," Evy said, "just to make sure."

The boys gave us plenty of warning when they arrived. They stampeded through the hall like a herd of cattle, laughing and teasing as they stomped up the steps. The clamor stopped abruptly when they got to our door. We could hear their loud whispers: "Knock on the door!"

"You knock, Steve."

"No, you go first. You knock."

There was shuffling. "Hey, don't push!" More laughter.

The girls giggled. "They're embarrassed," Evy said.

"It looks as though they'll never knock at the rate they're going." I went to the door and swung it open. Philly was hitting Moish on the head. "Act like a gentleman, Moish! Oh, hi, Leely!"

I waved them in. "You guys intend to spend the whole night out there deciding who should knock? We're not serving the pancakes in the hallway."

Grinning like nincompoops, they pushed one another toward the dining room. Their eyes flew wide open when they saw the streamers, balloons and the pretty table with the Hanukkah menorah in the center.

"Wow!" they sang out as they looked around.

"This is a real party!" Philly exclaimed.

"Of course it is! What did you expect? We only make real parties." I raised my nose, and the other girls did the same.

Noticing that Frankie was missing, Francy frowned and asked, "Where's Frankie?"

"He's coming. He's coming," Moish answered. "He said he'd meet us here."

A few minutes later Frankie arrived carrying something completely wrapped in brown paper. "Happy Hanukkah, Leely!" He held it out for me to take.

"For me? How come?" I was surprised. I looked at everybody and shrugged my shoulders. I had prepared myself to give a gift, not to receive one. I removed the paper. It was a flower pot with a plant I had never seen before. It had yellow flowers with large bright-red petals that looked like tree leaves.

"My grandfather sells these a lot in his nursery this time of year. My mom said it's proper to bring it to you for inviting me to your Hanukkah party."

"Gosh! It's a beautiful plant!" I said. "I've never seen one before. What's it called?"

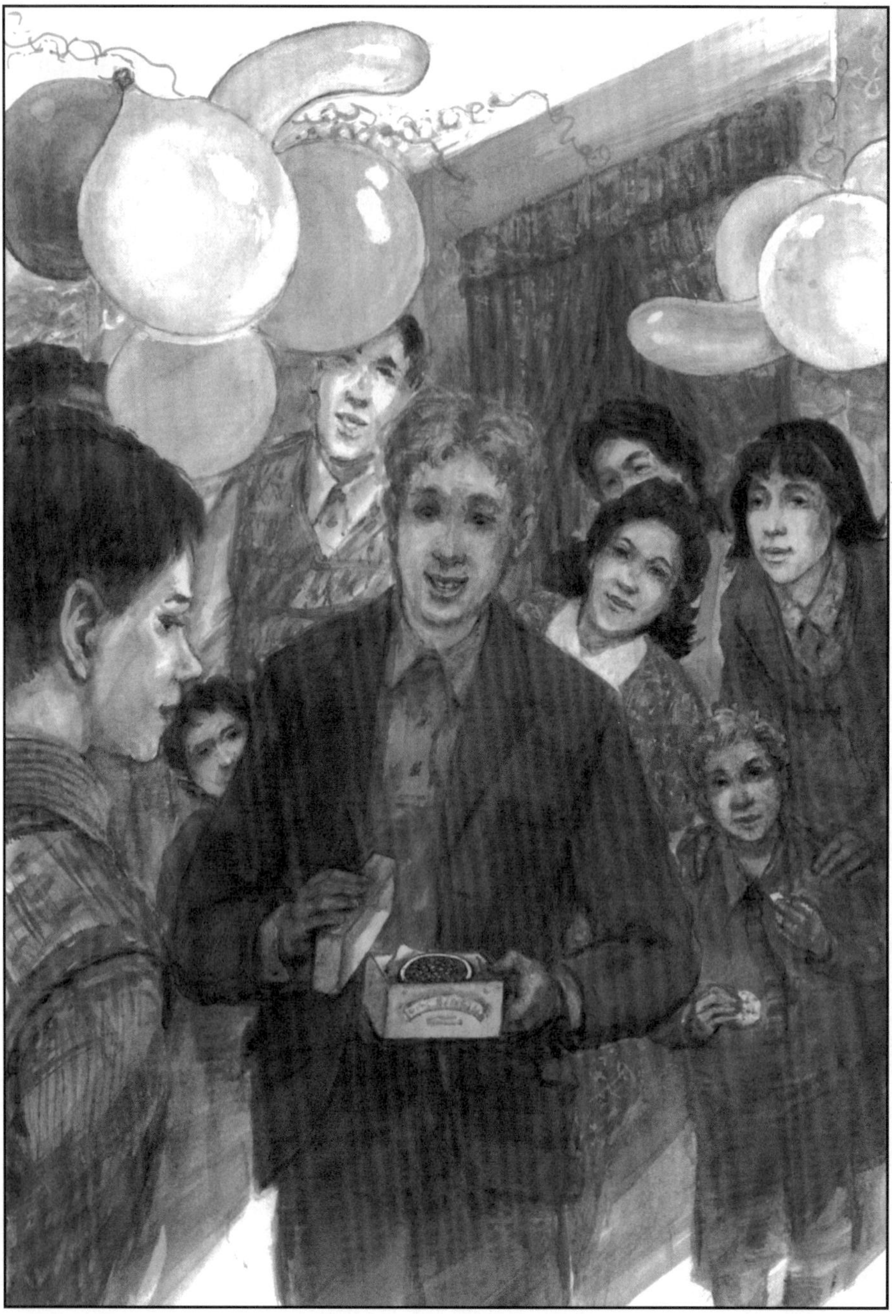

"Oh, I've seen it many times," Francy said. "It's called a poinsettia."

"That's right!" Frankie nodded. "It's a tropical plant. It comes from Mexico. That's why my mom made me wrap it good, so the cold wouldn't kill it."

"Gee, thank you! Thanks a lot!" Impressed with my Hanukkah present, I was all smiles as I placed it on the buffet next to Philly's present. I looked at the box and thought, Should I give it to him now? No. Everyone is not quite comfortable yet. I'll wait a little while longer.

There was some joshing and kidding around, and soon Philly asked, "Hey, Leely, how come you're having a Hanukkah party?"

That was my cue. I picked up the yellow box. "I thought a Hanukkah party would be a nice way to give you this." I handed him the box.

Philly's face turned red. "Hey! It's not my bar mitzvah party yet. What's this?"

"Open it and see," I said, looking at all the smiling faces.

"Wow! Philly's getting gifts from girls now," Moish teased as Philly unwrapped the box.

"So what, Moish?" Francy said. "Frankie gave Leely a gift, didn't he? It's nothing to laugh about. It's a very nice thing to do!"

Philly opened the box and looked in. "Holy cow!" he exclaimed. "Look at this great taillight!" He took the light out and held it up for all to see. "This is S-U-P-E-R!"

"Hey! Look how large it is!" Red said. "I ain't never seen any bike light that big before!" Red's eyes looked like lights themselves.

"Gee, Leely, this one's bigger than the one you broke! You didn't have to get such a large one, you know," Philly said, not looking too unhappy about it. "Geez, it's the greatest!"

Philly held it high, and everybody crowded around to see the light closer.

Everyone was so involved with Philly's light they never heard Yussy and his friends Donald and Freddie enter—until Yussy called out, "Holy Moses! That's big enough for a truck! I never saw a taillight that large on any bike! Let's have a look! It's a beauty!"

My eyes darted from the boys to Evy, who suddenly became interested in examining her shoes. These were the boy friends I had warned her not to invite. Did I know my sister! I was about to explode with anger, but I hid my rage because the guys were so excited about the light. Yussy said, "No kidding, Leely. Where did you find this? It's great!"

"At the Utica Avenue bike store. He doesn't keep it on the shelf with the others."

"Well, this is a gem! Really superb!" Donald said, taking the light and turning it at different angles. "You have good taste, Leely."

"Thank you," I said, "for making such a fuss over Philly's taillight. I'm sure these compliments are so I will let you stay for the party, even if you did come uninvited. What're you guys doing here anyway?"

Donald said, "The delicious aroma of your potato *latkes* drifted all the way over to Midwood Street, and our noses followed the whiff to its origin, when, to our surprise, *voilà!* We found ourselves right here."

I threw sharp dagger looks at Evy. Avoiding my eyes, she said as she turned away, "But I never, never mentioned the taillight to them. That's the truth!" She looked at Donald. "Isn't it, guys?"

"That's a fact," Donald said. "This is the first we know about the taillight. Honest!" Donald held up three fingers up in a Boy Scout salute.

"Ditto!" Yussy agreed.

"It's a surprise to me," Freddie said, examining the light.

Francy said, "Now I know why Evy kept grating so many potatoes."

"And why Barbara brought extra potatoes," I added. "They knew their friends were coming all along. You see what I mean? What did I tell you girls? My sister always has something up her sleeve. So now it's not only our party, it's theirs, too."

Philly picked up on it. "God forbid I have something with my own friends and big brother Yussy doesn't stick his nose in. If it were vice versa, you can bet they wouldn't let us crash their party."

"That's right. Like they didn't let us join their bonfire. We had to make our own," Red complained.

"Yeah! But ours turned out better," Francy said.

"You bet!" Moish said, sniffing the aroma of fried potatoes. "So where are the *latkes* already?"

"Okay, okay," Yussy said, "we heard about the party and just came up to see what a Hanukkah party looks like. That's all! If you're going to feel that way about it, give us a taste of the *latkes* and we'll get out of here."

I turned to my friends, "Do you want to eat first or play *dreidel* first?" I asked.

"Eat first!" everyone shouted.

"I'm dying to know what they taste like. I heard they're really good." Frankie had his fork ready in his hand.

"They are, Frankie," Francy said. "They really are."

"All right, but first we have to light the Hanukkah candles." I picked up the match I had prepared near the menorah. "Everyone chime in with the prayer."

"Light it from the left side first," Evy said. I threw her a don't-tell-me-what-to-do look.

"Today's the third day, so only three candles," Moish said.

"And don't forget the *shamos* first. Then use that to light the rest of the candles," Millie added.

"Jeepers, I know, I know!" I struck the match.

"You're lighting from the wrong end," Irene said.

"No, I'm not. You're looking at it from the opposite side. That's why it looks wrong. From where I'm standing it's the left side."

They all moved close to the menorah and chanted the prayer for lighting the candles. Except, of course, for Frankie and Francy, everyone seemed to know it. We sang out "*Happy Hanukkah!*"

"Okay, let's go! *Latke* time!" Philly shouted.

Evy and I piled the *latkes* on two platters. The boys were waiting, forks in hand and licking their lips, as we brought the pancakes in. Francy spooned out her applesauce, and Irene served the sour cream.

"These *latkes* look almost as beautiful as my taillight," Philly said, putting two pancakes on his plate.

Moish mumbled with a mouthful of hot pancakes, "On'y you can't eat a tai'yight."

"That's true." Philly bit into a pancake.

The real fun was beginning. The boys clowned and the girls started dancing the *hora* around the table—and we all sang:

> Oh Hanukkah, oh Hanukkah
> Come light the menorah.
> Come gather around
> We'll all dance the *hora*.
> Hot potato *latkes*
> Is what we will eat,
> Play spin the dreidel
> We'll give you a treat.

Then Donald said, "This is the time you're supposed to play spin the bottle for kisses."

Philly smiled mischievously and looked at me. "Yeah, lets! Hey, Leely, go get a milk bottle outside your door."

"No! Now don't start trouble! We're not gonna play any kissing games."

The words flew right out of my mouth. I didn't know why I said them. I did know my heart was beating faster.

"Why not?" Philly asked.

"Yeah, why not?" all the boys echoed.

I stared hard at Evy. "Ask my sister, she's the chaperon. If she permits it, we'll play."

Evy bit her lower lip and stared back at me. The room became quiet. Every face had a daring smile as we looked defiantly at Evy.

With half-closed eyes still staring at me, Evy's face turned pink. She said, "You can play spin the dreidel for candy instead of spin the bottle for kisses."

A loud moan swept through the room. "Ahhhhhh."

20. The Aftermath

I RAISED THE SHADE SO I COULD LOOK OUT THE WINDOW WHILE lying on my bed. It had started snowing. The falling flakes looked so pretty underneath the streetlight in front of our house.

I heard Evy turn in her bed. "You awake?" I asked.

"Yes, I can't seem to fall asleep."

"Me either."

"It's the party. I keep thinking about it." Evy took a deep breath. "The aftermath of a successful event."

"Yeah," I agreed. "It's the aftermath." We were quiet for a while.

"It's snowing." I broke the silence again.

"Mm. And very cold."

"Want to come into my bed? Bring your blanket, it'll be warmer."

With two blankets on us we felt the warmth immediately. We lay silently watching the snow fall.

"It was a good party, Leely. I would call it a great success."

"Do you really think so?"

"Absolutely! Everybody had fun. There was never a dull moment. Loads of laughter, too."

"I'm glad the boys agreed to spin the dreidel for candy, not kisses." I said.

"Me, too."

"And the *latkes* came out really good," I said, tasting them again in my mind. "Evy?"

"Mmmm?"

"Your friends are nice. They really aren't snobs. They were very helpful."

"Thanks!" Evy appreciated my changed opinion of her friends. "We're both lucky. In the short time we've been living here we've made some nice friends. You like Francy the best, though, don't you?"

"Oh, yes! She's my best friend. We have a special kind of friendship. We share a lot. We enjoy just spending time together—even if we only talk. My other friends are nice, too. But she's—she's more understanding."

Evy turned from her back to her side, facing me. "How about all that stuff with Millie? It's nice that you're friends again."

I nodded. "I feel guilty that I thought Millie took the money when all the time it was her mother. Boy, that woman is something! I think she's an embarrassment for Millie."

Evy changed the subject. "Philly was thrilled with the taillight. Such a nice surprise."

"Good! I wanted it to be a surprise. But boy, am I glad it's over with. For a while there it looked like I was never going to get that taillight. Now maybe I can concentrate on my bat mitzvah. It'll be more work than I originally expected."

"You can do it, Leely. If any girl in this neighborhood can become the first bat mitzvah, it's you. I'm proud you're my sister. "

"Thanks."

We were quiet again.

"Philly likes you," Evy said.

"I know."

Evy put her arm around my waist. "Guess what?" she whispered. "Donald asked me out on a date."

"No kidding? A real date?" I sat up in the bed.

"Uh-huh."

It was cold. I lowered myself back under the covers and faced Evy. "Like what kind of date? Where will you go? To the movies?"

"No, to the city."

"You mean Manhattan?"

"Yes. We're going to go to the Museum of Natural History and to the Planetarium. We'll leave in the morning and spend the whole day in the city."

"How exciting! I'm so thrilled for you, Evy. When are you going?"

"Next Sunday. I though he'd never get around to asking me anywhere other than the library."

"This is your first real date, Evy."

"I know. Isn't it great?" Evy smiled dreamily in the soft, dim light of the room.

"Yeah! It sure is." I felt happy for my sister.

Just then there was another whispering voice in the room. "Evy. Leely. We're cold." Arnie stood shivering at the foot of my bed. He was holding Malkah in his arms. His hair was tousled, and the buttons of his pajamas were unevenly fastened. He looked so small and cute.

"Oh, gosh. Of course you're cold," Evy said. "It's freezing out there. Get in."

I lowered the covers in the middle of the bed, and Malkah leapt in. We all laughed. Then Arnie slipped in between Evy and me.

"Oh, look!" Arnie said happily. "It's snowing."

We turned to the window to watch the snow. Malkah turned, too. With the covers tucked under our chins we were cuddled like four spoons in a drawer as our eyelids dropped slowly with the falling snow.

THE END

Glossary

A klug is mir!	Woe is me!
bimah	a platform in the synagogue on which the Torah is read
dreidel	spin toy
gelt	money
Gottenyoo!	Dear God!
kenubble	garlic
kenippel	money saved in a handkerchief tied with a knot
kinder	children
kreplach	stuffed pockets of dough like won ton or ravioli
kvetch	complain
latkes	potato pancakes
Mama Mia!	Mother mine!
mamele	darling daughter
Mio Dio!	My God!
mitzvah	good deed, commandment
meshugah	crazy

mondel brot	almond cake, toasted in hard slices
nu	well, so…
nu shoin	hurry, come on already
oy vey!	oh dear!
Shabbas	Sabbath, begins Friday at sundown and ends Saturday at sundown
shiva	mourning for seven days
shmutz	dirt
tatele	darling son
trope	cantilation marks for chanting Hebrew prayers and Torah reading
vey is mir!	woe to me!
yenta	gossip, busybody